Contemporary Chinese Poetry
in English Translation Series

Zhai Yongming
Selected Poems

Translated by Andrea Lingenfelter and others

教育部人文社会科学重点研究基地
安徽师范大学中国诗学研究中心 组编
Chinese Poetry Research Center of Anhui Normal University

杨四平 主编　　上海文化出版社

当代汉诗英译丛书

翟永明诗歌英译选

CONTENTS

目录

INTERLINEAR SPACE: A PRELUDE

Calmly plant the heart with a thousand slim bamboos.

Calmly sprinkle from a pail of fresh water.

Calmly change to a creeping snail.

Calmly turn the heart to a tea bowl.

If never born, how can you die?

If forever barefoot, why wear shoes?

If astride the sky, why set foot on earth?

If above the earth, why follow any path?

In fifty years, I'll be who?

In a hundred, who'll be me?

Stretch the tendons, flex the joints, renew, replace.

Hold one breath, live a lie.

Translated by Diana Shi & George O'Connell

行间距：一首序诗

从容地在心中种千棵修竹
从容地在体内洒一桶净水
从容地变成一只缓缓行动的蜗牛
从容地、把心变成一只茶碗

从来没有生过，何来死？
一直赤脚，何来袜？
在天上迈步，何来地？
在地上飞翔，何来道？

五十年后我将变成谁？
一百年后谁又成为我？

撑筋拔骨的躯体置换了
守住一口气　变成赝品人生

MOTHER

So many places one cannot reach, my feet ache, Mother. In the
    ravenous dawn
you never taught me how to be tinged with ancient sorrows.

My heart your heart, my blood yours, the pool
at sunrise where you find your own face, amazed.

You woke me to the noise of the world,
gave me birth, twin
to the world's misfortune.
So many years I couldn't recall this night's sobbing,

that ray of light which made you pregnant so far off, its beam
    uncertain
between life and death, your eyes owning the darkness.

How heavy the shadows that pass through our soles,
my smile in your arms and enigma.

Who knows how you led me through everything in innocence;
untouched, I still take the world as virginal.

Didn't my bright laughter
set summer a fire?

母亲

无力到达的地方太多了，脚在疼痛，母亲，你没有
教会我在贪婪的朝霞中染上古老的哀愁。我的心只像你

你是我的母亲，我甚至是你的血液在黎明流出的
血泊中使你惊讶地看到你自己，你使我醒来

听到这世界的声音，你让我生下来，你让我与不幸构成
这世界的可怕的双胞胎。多年来，我已记不得今夜的哭声

那使你受孕的光芒，来得多么遥远，多么可疑，站在生与死
之间，你的眼睛拥有黑暗而进入脚底的阴影何等沉重

在你怀抱之中，我曾露出谜底似的笑容，有谁知道
你让我以童贞方式领悟一切，但我却无动于衷

我把这世界当作处女，难道我对着你发出的
爽朗的笑声没有燃烧起足够的夏季吗？没有？

Deserted in this world, entirely alone, enfolded
in sad sunlight, when I bent over the world

did I know what I had left? Time ground me in its mill
until I saw myself as dust.

Oh mother, when at last I've grown silent
will you rejoice? My love unspoken,

some part of you bears this secret, my eyes
open wounds, staring through your pain.

Living for the sake of life, I court my own devastation
against primal love, one stone cast aside,

drying like marrow in the wind.
The orphans of this world

utterly reveal all blessings,
but who knows best

how any raised by mother's hands
will die at last from birth.

Translated by Diana Shi & George O'Connell

我被遗弃在世上，只身一人，太阳的光线悲哀地
笼罩着我，当你俯身世界时是否知道你遗落了什么？

岁月把我放在磨子里，让我亲眼看见自己被碾碎
呵，母亲，当我终于变得沉默，你是否为之欣喜

没有人知道我是怎样不着边际地爱你，这秘密
来自你的一部分，我的眼睛像两个伤口痛苦地望着你

活着为了活着，我自取灭亡，以对抗亘古已久的爱
一块石头被抛弃，直到像骨髓一样风干，这世界

有了孤儿，使一切祝福暴露无遗，然而谁最清楚
凡在母亲手上站过的人，终会因诞生而死去

THE BLACK ROOM

All crows under Heaven are equally black, and this
Fills me with fear, they have so many
Relatives, their numbers are legion, they're hard to resist

But we're indispensable, we three sisters
Slim and graceful, we glide to and fro
Looking like winners
But I intend to make mischief, I'm cruel at heart
Keeping up the appearance of a sweet-tempered daughter
My footsteps retrace my daily defeats

Awaiting proposals in our boudoirs, we young ladies of good
    family
Smile resentfully, racking our brains
For ways to enhance our charms
Youthful, beautiful, like fires ablaze
Seared black, single-minded snares
(Which of these good men with well-sharpened teeth, an
    unwavering gaze
And a steady expression will be my brother-in-law?)

黑房间

天下乌鸦一般黑，至此
我感到胆怯，它们有如此多的
亲戚，它们人多势众，难以抗拒

我们却必不可少，我们姐妹三人
亭亭玉立，来回踱步
胜券在握的模样
我却有意使坏，内心刻薄
表面保持当女儿的好脾气
重蹈每天的失败

待字闺中，我们是名门淑女
悻悻地微笑，挖空心思
使自己变得多姿多彩
年轻，貌美，如火如荼
炮制很黑，很专心的圈套
（哪些牙齿磨利，目光笔直的好人
毫无起伏的面容是我的姐夫？）

I sense

Our chamber beset on all sides

At night, cats and mice alike are stirring

And we go to sleep, searching our dreams for unknown house numbers

At night, we women are like ripe melons ready to fall from the vine

Conjugal bliss, and all of that

We three sisters, different with each new day

Marriage, still the crux of finding a mate

Lights in the bedroom fill newlyweds with disappointment

Risk it all on one throw, I tell myself

"Home is where the journey begins"

Translated by Andrea Lingenfelter

我感到
我们的房间危机四伏
在夜晚，猫和老鼠都醒着
我们去睡，在梦中寻找陌生的门牌号码
在夜晚，我们是瓜熟蒂落的女人
颠鸾倒凤，如此等等

我们姐妹三人，我们日新月异
婚姻，依然是择偶的中心
卧室的光线使新婚夫妇沮丧
孤注一掷，我对自己说
"家是出发的地方"

WHITE CORRIDOR

I've seen a small white passage

Flickering on sleepless nights

Gusty winds rustle and wrinkle my skirts

Droplets of blood flowering

Like the humdrum existence   of so many signatures

I've seen a sickly girl pale as jade draped across the bed

She turns her pretty face from side to side

Her fever's wellsprings shatter the summer heat

I run past a vanished door

Where a half-opened chest cavity

Has turned an arrogant heart

Into vital hopes

I've seen a lonely little passage

A woman in a white coat walking quietly in

The sound of her weeping carries

Mother's blood-covered hands appear and disappear

白色的走廊

我见过白色的小小走廊
在不眠之夜移动
衣裙吹皱沙沙作响的风
小小的血滴开着花
像很多签名　单单调调的存在

我见过玉体横陈的病女孩
把美貌的头转动
她高烧的理由把夏天的温度破坏
我跑过失踪的门
那儿半开半闭的胸膛
把内心的嚣张变成
一些活生生的愿望

Wavering before my eyes

Placing on me the burden of the afternoon

The brilliance of the scalpel

Tightly stitched rays of light

I've seen my mother's small passage

Awakened into darkness with a start

A life force like water gently held me up

That's how I was chased out

That's how a small, immaculate passage

Was rent apart   and I was pulled out

A sickly body has a botanical garden that's like a dream

A host of diseases has lodged there

Lacking origin or outcome

Indefatigable

Eyes stare at the rips in white clothing

Full of allure

The sickly girl of summer feels her way forward

Meek and mild   her snowy gaze

Has a vision of everything swept clean

Translated by Andrea Lingenfelter

我见过孤独的小小走廊
穿白罩衫的女人悄悄走来
她哭泣的声音传得很远
母亲沾满血迹的两手忽隐忽现
在我眼中逡巡
让我担负起一个下午
手术刀的光芒
以及密密缝合的光线

我见过母亲的小小走廊
在黑暗中惊醒
似水的生命力把我轻轻托起
这是被迫出逃的方式
这是纯洁的小小走廊
分裂的方式　拖着我
病体有如梦中的百草园

栖息着多种多样的疫疾
没有来龙去脉
没有困倦
眼睁睁看着白衣的裂纹
充满魔力
夏天的病女孩摸索着走来
温顺的　雪白的凝眸
带着扫荡一切的幻觉

THE CHANGING ROOM

Four corners   passing time inside four curtained corners
flowing dresses slit so high
their fish tails swishing side to side
My changing room   tier after tier of
little dolls ensconced   their
fragile pupils violently
fasten onto the goldfish bowl   catch
me strolling by   amethyst crystals embrace the draft
another kind of skin

Ever-changing old-fashioned dress, how it guards my
chilly hauteur   I'm thin as kindling
In these four corners   hungry women gorge on
soiled colors   gulping down gallons of liquid
a woman's full lunar eclipse
Let me lift my head (Time and tide
ravage these delicate brows)   The changing room gives me
Something   has us form a line
as if we were lining up to enter Heaven

Never-changing red dress
a friend slips it onto   me blood red from head to toe
costumed for a mad dance
My friend's black pleated blouse
conceals wracking sobs behind stylized tears

更衣室

四个墙角　蹲着四角布帘
款款开衩的裙衫
随同它们的鱼尾摆
我的更衣室　层层叠叠
坐着小玩偶　它们
易碎的瞳孔狂暴地
揪住金鱼缸　瞧
我走来　紫水晶抱住一团风
那才是别样的肌肤

百变的古典长裙呵护我的
神情冷落　别样的骨瘦如柴
在这四角　贪食的女人吞掉
肮脏的色彩　吞掉成吨的液体
它们是女人的月全食
让我抬起头来（沧桑
脆弱的额头）　更衣室为我
付出什么　让我们排队
如同排队上天堂

不变的红色连衣裙
女友为我披上　一身如血的
狂舞之妆
女友的黑色褶皱衫
把暴戾藏于哭泣的方式中

and it's fine   needles, bandages, a few pieces of jade
like talismans blessed with maternal love   attached to
the superstitious ones who never go out of style
It's all right   like a horde of spiders
we cover the printed curtains   we have our uses
in the changing room   dressing up our bold plans

In my little changing room
I change my gender, bones and hair, down to the roots
A listless voice reads a children's book:
"One winter morning, there was a great fire…
acetylene racing and slapping the wind
scarlet on the snow wounded me"

My quicksilver ritualistic eye contact
has been eaten by the habitual universe
My classmates threaten me   their piercing looks
like screeches from each of their mouths
In my little changing room
I alter my figure, my gestures, my vacuous smile
and listen to a man reading a children's book:
"The anxious school   the anxious
road home   My mother standing before me
like a gift in a shop window…"

还好　针尖　绑带和一些玉石
像母爱的避邪之物　粘住
永不过时的迷信一族
还好　我们蜘蛛般爬满
印花布帘　我们有了用途
在更衣室　妆成大胆的图案

在我小小的更衣室
我变换性别、骨头和发根
沉闷的嗓音在念儿童读物：
　"一个冬天的早晨、一场火灾……
奔跑的乙炔扑打风
雪地上的红色伤了我"

我变来变去的注目礼
被万事万物的依旧吃掉
同学们威胁我　那些目光
像一张张嘴的尖叫
在我小小的更衣室
我变换身材、手势和憨笑
听见一个男人在念儿童读物：
　"揪心的学校　揪心的
回家的路　母亲站在面前
像橱窗内的礼物……"

Black cloth shoes changed in and out of
burst open by the long ant trail of Time
Sleeplessness at siesta   exchanged for
a night of growth   My classmates
watch me   their broken smiles
blocking my exits

In my little changing room
I alter my come-hither glances, downy skin and scent
someone is reading a children's book in the dark:
"The weeping emergency   room the terror of flames
takes root in my skin   the shriek of the radio
invades my ears   the paper-thin years of childhood..."
The changing yet unchanging world finds me   comforts me
Verdant trees at school grow much faster than I do
My classmates   surround me
altogether their eyes   are larger
clearer   brighter than   mine

In my little changing room
I change my hairstyle, lingerie, and blood type
My voice is high and clear   I read a children's story:
"The sorrowful apple   the stolen cheeks of childhood
A voice shouts out from the crowd:
Mother, O Mother   it's time to say goodbye"

换来换去的黑色布鞋
被蚂蚁般增长的时间撑破
午睡时的不眠　换来
一夜间的生长　同学们
看着我　他们破坏性的微笑
让我找不到自救

在我小小的更衣室里
我变换眼波、汗毛和体味
黑暗中有人在念儿童读物：
　"哭泣的急救室　火焰的恐惧
植入皮肤　还有收音机的嘶叫
浸进耳膜　这脆若薄纸的幼年……"
变和不变的世界找到我　安慰我
青青校树的生长比我快得多
同学们　围着我
他们全体的眼睛　比我的眼睛
大　比我清　以及灿烂

在我小小的更衣室
我变换发式、内衣和血型
我的高音清脆　念着儿童读物：
　"伤心的苹果　偷走的童年脸颊
人丛里有一个声音喊：
母亲啊母亲　离别就在眼前"

The constantly moving household changes like the seasons

Every time you turn around it's time to mortgage "the past"

My classmates abandon grammar   sowing disorder

    with sets of metal teeth

Four walls and corners   passing time in four curtained corners

all this stuff fashioned from wasted grief

Gazing at my naked back   stiff waist and

the gaping mouths of little dolls   I might

float up with the bubbles in that four-cornered

fish bowl   and watch the married people

within the four walls of this house   the cookery and small talk

Seeing even farther   under the eaves of these four-sided

    courtyards

searching all night for that frightening lamplight

and a sense of human figures behind the windows

My little changing room   When depression comes to call

this is where I sleep   When people call me "clumsy"

this is where I sleep   these gray-green clothes

these gentle gray-green eyes   these silken gray-green

substances annoint my body   heavy clouds of vapor

cut me off from the outside world   this sleep from another era

so distant and deep

Translated by Andrea Lingenfelter

搬来搬去的家像季节变换
转眼就到了典卖"过去"的日子
同学们离开语法　和捣乱的金属牙套

四个墙角　蹲着四角布帘
它们是空空哀愁制成的材料
注视我的赤裸　腰部的僵硬和
小小玩偶的张口结舌　我可以和
四角玻璃缸里的鱼泡
同时升起　看房子四周那些
已结婚的人　烹调和谈天

看更远处　四方屋檐下
整夜追逐恐惧的灯光
与人形的隔窗之感
我的小小更衣室　当沮丧来临
我在这里睡眠　当有人说我"笨拙"
我在这里睡眠　这些灰绿色的衣衫
这些灰绿色的温柔眼睛　这些灰绿色
软性的东西敷我　绵绵的氤氲
把我和门外隔开　我的隔世之感
宜深宜远

ABANDONED HOUSE

There, the steps are a deep purple
There, the plants are red sunbirds
There, the stones have human faces

I often pass by there
In a variety of nervous postures
I've always been feeble come dusk
And that abandoned house shuts its eyes tight
As I stand and stare
Watching rays of daylight slide from its body in agony

Muttering to myself, my heart racing
My footsteps circle, while the nameless and contagious sorrow
Shooting from the rooftop passes through my brain
Like a name too lofty to reach
Like a gift savored in solitary splendor or a painting
Like a piece of glass sparkling with refinement but heavy with death

荒屋

那里有深紫色台阶
那里植物是红色的太阳鸟
那里石头长出人脸

我常常从那里走过
以各种紧张的姿态
我一向在黄昏时软弱
而那里荒屋闭紧眼睛
我站在此地观望
看着白昼痛苦的光从它身上流走

念念有词，而心忐忑
脚步绕着圈，从我大脑中走过
房顶射出传染性的无名悲痛
像一个名字高不可攀
像一件礼物孤芳自赏和一幅画
像一块散发着高贵品质的玻璃死气沉沉

There, everything is like a rumor

And heats truck lamps offer their conspiracies

There, it will be proven: nothing more will remain

I arrive   I approach   I trespass

Nursing a temperament I've never revealed

Living like an urn filled with ashes

Its proud days lie buried in dust, untouched

And just like this abandoned house

I am myself

Translated by Andrea Lingenfelter

那里一切有如谣言
那里有害热病的灯提供阴谋
那里后来被证明：无物可寻

我来了　我靠近　我侵入
怀着从不开敞的脾气
活得像一个灰瓮

它的傲慢日子仍然尘封未动
就像它是荒屋
我是我自己

MARGINS

Six in the evening, the setting sun blazes

Across your coupled limbs

Staring into the cloudy eyes of a madman

You could fight back, but I've had my fill of

The wind's sobbing, and no one will notice a grain of sand

Staring fixedly at the two of you, it's trying to say

The birds are once again repeating an old refrain

You two have walked to the margins of the stars

You know the meaning of silence

The strangeness of two names savoring autumn

You cover your tracks, denying me

Even a vestige of peace, while up in the sky grinning bats

Converse in a language not entirely human

边缘

傍晚六点钟，夕阳在你们
两腿之间燃烧
睁着精神病人的浊眼
你可以抗议，但我却饱尝
风的啜泣，一粒小沙并不起眼
注视着你们，它想说
鸟儿又在重复某个时刻的旋律

你们已走到星星的边缘
你们懂得沉默
两个名字的奇异领略了秋天
你们隐藏起脚步，使我
得不到安宁，蝙蝠在空中微笑
说着一种并非人类的语言

You couldn't possibly make a prettier picture

Than you do tonight, your head

Pillowed on his lap, the way

Water is cradled by stones

Now you believe the loneliest moments

Will ripen into grapes, turning translucent when they should

    turn translucent

Bursting when they should burst

The blinded pool wants to see right through the night, the moon like

A cat's eye, and I'm neither pleased nor aggrieved

Leaning against a dead fence and staring at you both

I want to tell you   No one is holding back the night

Darkness is already encroaching on these margins

Translated by Andrea Lingenfelter

这个夜晚无法安排一个
更美好的姿态，你的头
靠在他的腿上，就像
水靠着自己的岩石
现在你们认为无限寂寞的时刻
将化为葡萄，该透明的时候透明
该破碎的时候破碎

瞎眼的池塘想望穿夜，月亮如同
猫眼，我不快乐也不悲哀
靠在已经死去的栅栏上注视你们
我想告诉你　没有人去拦阻黑夜
黑暗已进入这个边缘

PREMONITION

A woman dressed in black arrives in the dead of night

Just one secretive glance leaves me spent

I realize with a start: this is the season when all fish die

And every road is criss-crossed with traces of birds in flight

A corpse-like chain of mountain ranges dragged off by the darkness

The heartbeats of nearby thickets barely audible

Enormous birds peer down at me from the sky

With human eyes

In a barbarous atmosphere that keeps its secrets

Winter lets its brutally male consciousness rise and fall.

I've always been uncommonly serene

Like the blind, I see night's darkness in the light of day

Artless as an infant, my fingerprints

Can reveal no more grief

Footsteps! A sound now growing old

Dreams seem to possess some knowledge, and with my own eyes

I saw an hour that forgot to blossom

Press down on the dusk.

Fresh moss in their mouths, the meanings they sought

Folded their smiles back into their breasts in tacit understanding

The night seems to shudder, like a cough

Stuck in the throat, I've already quit this dead end hole.

Translated by Andrea Lingenfelter

预感

穿黑裙的女人黉夜而来
她秘密的一瞥使我精疲力竭
我突然想起这个季节鱼都会死去
而每条路正在穿越飞鸟的痕迹

貌似尸体的山峦被黑暗拖曳
附近灌木的心跳隐约可闻
那些巨大的鸟从空中向我俯视
带着人类的眼神
在一种秘而不宣的野蛮空气中
冬天起伏着残酷的雄性意识

我一向有着不同寻常的平静
犹如盲者，因此我在白天看见黑夜
婴儿般直率，我的指纹
已没有更多的悲哀可提供
脚步！正在变老的声音
梦显得若有所知，从自己的眼睛里
我看到了忘记开花的时辰
给黄昏施加压力

藓苔含在口中，他们所恳求的意义
把微笑会心地折入怀中
夜晚似有似无地痉挛，像一声咳嗽
憋在喉咙，我已离开这个死洞

DESIRE

Tonight all the lights are shining for you
Tonight you are a small colonial outpost
You've lingered here, and melancholy seeps
From your body, with tiny, perfect drops of water

Like a clean bright ball of scented flesh, the moon
Sleeps sweetly, each breath a seduction
A night squeezed between two days
And in their midst, the black orbs of your eyes
Still filled with joy

What kind of commotion was heaped together to shape my body
Beyond consolation, feeling like some substance about to take form
The walls in the dream turn black
Making you see the shadows overflowing the triangle
Every pore on your body opens up
Concepts you cannot grasp
Stars in the night sky glimmer inhumanly
But your eyes are flooded
With the sorrows and joys of antiquity

Bearing the wounds of contentment
Your beautiful gaze possesses a demonic power
That transforms this moment into a memory that can't be wiped away

Translated by Andrea Lingenfelter

渴望

今晚所有的光只为你照亮
今晚你是一小块殖民地
久久停留，忧郁从你身体内
渗出，带着细腻的水滴

月亮像一团光洁芬芳的肉体
酣睡，发出诱人的气息
两个白昼夹着一个夜晚
在它们之间，你黑色眼圈
保持着欣喜

怎样的喧嚣堆积成我的身体
无法安慰，感到有某种物体将形成
梦中的墙壁发黑
使你看见三角形泛滥的影子
全身每个毛孔都张开
不可捉摸的意义
星星在夜空毫无人性地闪耀
而你的眼睛装满
来自远古的悲哀和快意

带着心满意足的创痛
你优美的注视中，有着恶魔的力量
使这一刻，成为无法抹掉的记忆

GIVE ME LOVE, I'LL LOVE HIM

Much sickness in much drink.
I choose it.
Pretty poison. Looking at you,
who'll offer my last glory?

Some insist on making
libations everywhere.
Some just taste the mouthfuls
sliding down—relaxed, happy.

Pretty poison means the place
drink can't take you.
No matter how you hope,
you still need others.
Even if you try to heal yourself
you hurt.

给我爱情，我就爱他

很多的病　很多的醉里
我选择它
美丽的毒　看看你
就要给我临终的辉煌

有些人　非得要把酒
酾向四面八方
有些人　集中为入喉的一口
他们都心旷神怡
他们都享受

美丽的毒　就是你的醉意
达不到的地方
就是你无论如何帮助自己
也需要别人的地方
就是你拼命治疗
也会让你痛一痛的地方

That's the danger walking backward step by step,

excruciation haunting your soul.

That's honey we fry in joy,

slathering our lips,

last taste of lost dessert.

Give me love, I'll love him.

Give me flowers, I'll smell sweet.

Give me summer, I'll shine.

Go charmingly, go mad.

Go irrigate, go die.

Stare at the sky for a harvest.

Translated by Diana Shi & George O'Connell

它就是一步一回首的危险
它就是灵魂缠绕的酷刑
它就是我们尽情地煎
充分地抹上蜜糖
最后一口吞掉　泻完的甜点

给我爱情　我就爱他
犹如给我花　我就香
给我夏天　我就明亮

去动人　或去疯癫吧
去灌溉　或去死吧
它们都是望天收

1999.10.6

REVOLVING

It's not just the sun that revolves
The sinking started long ago, when I was born, upside down
The struggle was terrifying, and it shaped me
Maintaining this face-down reality, I've grown to the age that I have

I was no star when I arrived
I stand very still, while the road twists and turns
From East to West, there's no escaping the circle of Fate
But enough of that, for soon my head will be put into orbit
With my own eyes I see it cast into the sky
Where it fights that weightlessness with all of its strength

Earth presses down onto my feet, a heavy sky
Destroys me, it's that wheel spinning
Geraniums are too much like my heart, hot-blooded and slim
But I can't stop, can't stop it from turning
And finally there's a smile, like a fatal blow

Night or day? It's all the same
An eye that hatches oval stones, male and female bodies
They say the kohlrabi has flowered and withered already
But at the edge of the road
Black whirlpools are spinning into infinity

Revolving and revolving, like an
Unlucky star dancing in the air
Round and round, encircling me, but who is on your outer surface?

Translated by Andrea Lingenfelter

旋转

并非只是太阳在旋转
沉沦早已开始，当我倒着出生
这挣扎如此恐怖，使我成形
保存这头朝地的事实我已长得这般大

我来的时候并不是一颗星
我站得很稳，路总在转
从东到西，无法逃脱圆圈的命运
够了，不久我的头被装上轨道
我亲眼注视着它向天空倾倒
并竭力保持自身的重量

大地压着我的脚，一个沉重的天
毁坏我，是那轮子在晕旋
天竺葵太像我的心，又细腻又热情
但我无法停下来，使它不再转
微笑最后到来，像一个致命的打击

夜还是白昼？全都一样
孵出卵石之眼和雌雄之躯
据说球茎花已开得一无所剩
但靠着那条路的边缘
黑色涡旋正茫茫无边

旋转又旋转，像一颗
飞舞着不祥事件的星
把我团团围住：但谁在你的外端？

IN THE END I COME UP SHORT

Compared to my tongue my spirit
Runs fast   my hands
Are flightier and more fretful   than my heart

So let's all get up and sing
A quartet

And here comes someone to keep us in tune
It was a perfectly fine day
And you came along and killed my voice
Taking it from a soft murmur   to a ragged drone
You've made me come up short

Now it's my turn to perform!
Me and my beloved melody
Pouring out   we will
Copy down a piece of gold

终于使我周转不灵

我的灵魂比我的舌头
跑得快　我的手
比我的心　敏感善变

就让我们来演奏
四重唱吧

又来了一个人校音

好端端的一整天
你谋杀了我的嗓子
从温柔的资讯　到沙哑的排练
你终于使我周转不灵

现在轮到我来演奏！
我和我心爱的旋律
滔滔不绝　我们要
拷贝一片黄金

I want to reshape my soul

Into something bonier

I want to catch my rushing breath

As it comes and goes

I want to keep up with the even cadences of your words

Want you to believe in the sound of mine

And   in the sixth sense I have for my beloved

You've made me come up short in the end

Translated by Andrea Lingenfelter

我要修理我的灵魂
让它更骨感
我要抓住我的呼吸跑动
离开和回来
我要追赶你的吐字均匀
还要你相信我的发音
和   对恋人的第六感应

你终于使我周转不灵

PORTRAIT

1

Your ever reserved smile has dimmed
yet once again it has changed   the way it fools others'
    oblivious eyes
we were all wrong, it is only out of habit that water
slowly flows into the form of a thing

You're never calculating, more tolerant than most
devastating eyes will complete your masterpiece
as the autumn enjoys you   it's unsettled
the sun shines, but for its own reasons
and not for you   you know only how to love
but not how to be loved

2

You   merely yourself   displease others on first sight
you shouldn't come here when you're bored
your hair is too long, too threatening   leaving or arriving
you look like those risk-taking roots   dark and carefree
it should have been green waves   in a neurotic ocean
that restored your vitality
but now you're a wolf
happy, lively, vengeful teeth
bare themselves to the night, in the painting
your hatred seems so lonely   others praise it

肖像

1

你一向拘谨的微笑已杳
但又改换方式　使别人不自觉的眼光
再次领受欺骗
我们都想错了，水只是因为习惯
才慢慢流成某个东西的形状

你从不计算，比许多人要宽容
毁灭性的眼睛将完成你的代表作
秋天享受你时　感到不安
太阳发亮，是因为自己内部的原因
不是因为你　你只会爱
却不会被爱

2

你　只是你　第一次看见就让人不快
无聊的时辰你不该走来
过于长、过于威胁的头发　去或来
你都像那冒险的根　黝黑而自在
本该是绿色波浪　在神经质的大海里
恢复你充满生命的模样
现在却是一只狼
快乐、生动而复仇的牙齿
向着黑夜张开，在画中
你的恨也显得如此孤独　被人称道

3

And so it's the expected picture
but believe this: born illusory
consuming sweets   knowing the flavor of winter
you move this way and that   seeking a more remote posture
the tiny head seems to sink and float
implanting wherever it likes in the canvas
her passive variations   absentmindedly taking shape
tongue curled ever so slightly in the night sky
opening slightly   with the taste of death
at the beginning   at the beginning there was a human shape
possessed by her   you two became one
a bird cannot escape its own echo

4

For a short while   there were wild adventures
that made her incurable eyes widen with awe
utterly composed, but as her face held firm her heart was weak
she saw the heavy yoke of fate   and it's many wheel-shafts
and still doggedly endured   head in hand
like the pupil who surpasses the teacher
you stare at yourself   and see that she has no escape

3

因此一副期待的样子
但相信：生来多么虚幻
嚼食甜物　知道冬天的滋味
你移来移去　寻找更偏僻的姿势
小小的头若沉若浮
随遇而安地嵌入布中
她消极地变化　恍惚成形的样子
舌头微微卷起在夜空
微微开启　满嘴死亡的味道
最初　最初已有人形
附体于她　你们合二为一
鸟儿也逃不过自己的回声

4

有一刻　酿成旷世奇遇
使她病入膏肓的眼睛为之倾倒
不动声色　但又外厉内荏的表情
她看着命运的重轭　套着定数的辕
咬紧牙关　手支撑着头
青出于蓝的样子
你凝视自己　看她怎样在劫难逃

5

Perfectly average   but believing yourself a genius
painting uses its degenerate devices   to enrapture you
To what end? That limpid posture is so human
fragrant and warm   like the child of sweet osmanthus
you   are still you   distinct from any marvels
there then not there   vaporizing your sole ambition

Perfectly average   but you can't resist
can't confess, can't cure yourself
exceedingly pompous   my mother's arrogant girl
fervent   resentful   and in the end just falling apart

6

Fond of the cold   fond of the colors of night
you say to the painter   you're sitting oddly
off-kilter   your line of sight is unbalanced
what is tranquility? Tranquility is the motion you imagine
look over your shoulder   learn from painful experience
you will be content down to your bones

5

天资平平　又大愚若智
绘画以一次堕落方式　迷你
为了什么？那粼粼身姿也充满人性
芬芳暧昧　如同木樨树的后裔
你　仍是你　与一切奇迹无关
如隐如现　挥发仅有的锐气

天姿平平　你却无法抵御
无法交代也无法治愈
趾高气扬之至　是我母亲的傲慢女儿
慷慨　愤懑　最终自己崩溃

6

喜欢冷　喜欢黑夜那种颜色
你对画家说　你坐着的样子很古怪
歪着　使一切视线失去平衡
宁静是什么？宁静就是你设想的动作
扭过头来　痛定思痛
你感到彻骨的满足

7

Overwhelming color in a clenched hand
transformed day after day into a silent storm
a production that surprises you   though familiar and ancient
in this our only world   you are absolutely singular
look at yourself   as resolutely as you look at others
another head   another hand   float in the darkness
like pursuing soldiers drawing nearer
you suddenly think: this afternoon, this overcast day
have turned gloomy just for you

8

You're saying: she's been through a lot in life
and goes on living   her face is smooth as a stack of gifts
and even her enemies will be moved by her   unless
the terror preserved in your eyes   slowly fades

You're with her   she's with your heart
the body's most dangerous configuration   that brush
first painted your eyes
then painted the indiscernible parts
no one understands those secrets she can never salvage
and no one can escape her all-season stare

Translated by Gu Ailing（顾爱玲）

7

销魂的颜料在紧握的手中
一天天变成无言的风暴
惊异自己的产生　既熟悉又古老
在唯一的世界里　你绝对单一
看着自己　像看别人一样坚定
另外的头　另外的手　在暗处浮起
如同追兵已接近
你突然想起：这个下午这个阴天
是为你才黯淡的

8

你是说：她曾历经沧桑
生者如斯　脸部光滑好像一桩礼物
为此敌人也将被她打动　除非
你眼睛里始终保存的恐惧　慢慢消失

你同她　她同你的心
是体内最危险的组成　那支笔
先画你的眼
再画那些看不见的部分
无人理解她不可挽回的隐秘
也无人逃得过她春夏秋冬的凝视

1986.10

THE TESTAMENT OF HU HUISHAN

— With gratitude to Uncle Liu Jiakun who built

a memorial to Hu Huishan;

but who will make memorials

for all my classmates?

Where do they lie   I cannot find them

No one remains who knows their names

They too had mothers and fathers   mothers and fathers who also

      burned like flames

They too had umbilical cordsumbilical cords that took their

      parents' lives

Winding towards the ground

They too had milk teeth   but no one remains to save them

There won't be another school   where we might study

It's gone forever   and it's not in Heaven

Nor is there a mother or father to weep for me

They're gone forever   and they're not in Heaven

This is the longest fissure on the face of the earth

It swallowed us all   and all that remains

Are huge numbers   numbers large enough to make an even greater

      number of people weep

When the grade of concrete used for my memorial

Is better than that of my school could my frail body

Lift up the mighty earth

Could I turn my body   and release energy from underground

So people on the surface would see

Translated by Andrea Lingenfelter

胡慧姗自述

　　——感谢刘家琨叔叔
　　　　修建了胡慧姗纪念馆
　　　　我的同学谁来纪念？

他们躺在何处　我找不着
他们的名字再也无人知道
他们也有父母　父母也像火焰般燃烧
他们也有脐带　脐带把父母的命
往地下缠绕
他们一样也有乳牙　再也无人收藏

再也没有第二所学校　能让我们入读
再也没有　天堂里也没有
再也没有人间父母为我流泪
再也没有　天堂里也没有

这是世界上最长的裂缝
把我们一并吞下　剩下的
只有数字庞大　大到让更大数目的人流泪

当纪念我的水泥标号
超过学校　我瘦小的身体
能否把强壮的大地抬起
我能否翻个身　把地底的能量送出去
让上面的人看到

HER POINT OF VIEW

From one side of the bed, her point of view
Looking through the opposite side   watching your body
Emerging from a heap of clothing   cell phone   shoes
And keys

And let's not forget your fingers
They're long, slender   and straight
It's as if we could hear once again
The collision of hipbones and daylight

Everyone's been desexed
Everyone's unhealthy
Everyone's exposed outside their flesh

The place you're headed is a slough of despond
Even your suit of armor cannot
Protect your pressure points this time
Every square inch of your skin
Will grow slack in the end   Perhaps a little stroking
Might give her some pleasure as well

她的视点

她的视点从床的一端
射向另一端　看着你的身体
从一大堆衣服　手机　鞋
和钥匙中钻出来

还有你的指头
它们修长　刚直
似乎能再次听见
骨盆和白昼的碰撞声

每个人都被阉割了
每个人的健康都遗失了
每个人都暴露在他的肉体之外

要去的地方是个苦难窝
即使穿上盔甲　此时也不能
把你的穴道包裹起来
你的每一寸肌肤终究会
清淡起来　可供抚摸
她也会为此快活一番

Turn out the lights   The climax of evolutionary theory repeats

    ad nauseam:

What you're about to offer up tonight

Isn't that important as far as she's concerned

(Their child could witness

The entire process of procreation

Amniotic fluid   blood   baby

As it all comes splashing out there's

Nothing left behind, not one drop of semen

Nothing left behind, no space to call a haven)

Translated by Andrea Lingenfelter

关灯吧　进化论的高潮一再说：
你今晚准备献出来的
不是那么重要　对她而言

（他们的孩子会看见
生育的全过程
羊水　血　婴儿
唏里哗啦地冲出来
没留下一滴精子可供选择
没留下一寸空间可供栖息）

ESCAPING ALONE

Without having to look in all directions   your
fragrance will float out everywhere   If you want
to escape alone   an assassin will arrive here

When your body is light and longing for flight   there's no need
to cut off the wings of birds
and no need to be right next to love
Old and new games don't need to
be indulged in

Eventually you must depart from a close place
It's only from the closest place   that you can look out in the distance
The desire to leave is like water   it will evaporate
in the human world   A body that's alone
will also evaporate in some moment

What remains   is time
the slowness of seeing through rocks
the judo of loneliness

These three in one   pass through clouds and break through fog
Wanting to hold hands with you   wanting
to become the shield you cannot avoid

Translated by Jami Proctor Xu

孤身的逃

不用四处张望　你就会
在这世界里飘香　你想要
孤身的逃　就会有刺客来到

当你身轻想飞　也不必
去剪鸟类的翅膀
也不必去傍上爱
新与旧的老把戏　也不必
太沉湎

终于还是要从近处去
从最近处　才能望到远
去意象水　它就要在人间里
蒸发了　孤身的身
也要在某个时刻蒸发

剩下的　就是时间了
就是把石头看穿的缓慢了
就是孤独的柔道了

它们三位一体　穿云破雾
就要与你共执双手　就要
成为你无法避开的掩护了

1999.8.17

THE FIRST MONTH

Xinchou, Earth

Illness and early death

Spring Sacrifice to the Earth: February 16

As if it had been there all along, as if by prior arrangement
I arrived, and a voice beyond my control
Placed me in a south-facing wing

I arrived just in time for the pitch black days
Every footpath looked the same
Breezes chilled me pale and lonely
While the cornfields pulsed with energy
When I arrived, I heard the roaring of Pisces
And the endless trembling of the sensitive night

Tiny haystacks spread out in a solemn array
One feeble cloud, like a solitary wild animal
Moved in on tiptoe, with a taste of foul weather
As if meeting me gave it a heart to match its shape

第一月

　　——辛丑土
　　闭蛰
　　春社：二月十六日

仿佛早已存在，仿佛早已就序
我走来，声音概不由己
它把我安顿在朝南的厢房

第一次来我就赶上漆黑的日子
到处都有脸型相像的小径
凉风吹得我苍白寂寞
玉米地在这种时刻精神抖擞
我来到这里，听到双鱼星的嗥叫
又听见敏感的夜抖动不已

极小的草垛散布肃穆
脆弱唯一的云像孤独的野兽
蹑足走来，含有坏天气的味道
如同与我相逢成为值得理解的内心

Fishing poles gliding over the water, flickering oil lamps

Fierce and ragged, the barking of dogs plunges me into thought

Yesterday's howling wind seemed to comprehend everything

To say nothing of those black trees

Murderous traps are set in every corner

I've endured the moment that covered my body

And can now become moonlight, unfettered

A husband and wife hear the sound of pre-dawn rain in their dreams

Black donkeys lean against a millstone, talking about tomorrow

There, the soil where yin and yang intermingle

Knows each year by heart

I hear a cock's crow

And a windlass drawing water from a well

Translated by Andrea Lingenfelter

Xinchou refers to a time in the traditional Chinese calendar, spanning the first and second months of the lunar year, from Xiaohan in the first month to Lichun in the second month（1月小寒到2月立春）

鱼竿在水面滑动，忽明忽灭的油灯
热烈沙哑的狗吠使人默想
昨天巨大的风声似乎了解一切
不要容纳黑树
每个角落布置一次杀机
忍受布满人体的时刻
现在我可以无拘无束地成为月光

已婚夫妇梦中听见卯时雨水的声音
黑驴们靠着石磨商量明天
那里，阴阳混合的土地
对所有年月了如指掌

我听见公鸡打鸣
又听见辘轳打水的声音

THE SECOND MONTH

From dawn to noon, I cover the whole village on foot
My steps obeying a voice from beneath the ground
That brings me to the very depths of silence

No matter whose gate I come up to, someone is standing there
With a rice bowl in their hands, and someone is rocking an empty cradle
Passing wall after wall, my feet don't touch the ground
The abandoned houses there, boundless in their cruelty, coated in fine red
　　dust
What blocks my sympathetic gaze?
On a path where ants are sure to die
People are walking, their faces covered with leaves
All of the sunflowers have had their heads lopped off. Their coarse,
defiled necks
Stretch beneath the sky like a row of lies
A cape made of straw masquerades as a god, ready for a night of wicked
　　deeds

Shouts ring out during the Cold Food festival
To comfort the dead, the villagers exercise restraint
I keep searching, wearing my ever-failing smile
The wound in my heart is strung on the same thread as their naked eyes
How can I ever be part of Tranquil Village?
Each day brings more drowned babies and brides who swallow poison

第二月

从早到午，走遍整个村庄
我的脚听从地下的声音
让我到达沉默的深度

无论走到哪家门前，总有人站着
端着饭碗，有人摇着空空的摇篮
走过一堵又一堵墙，我的脚不着地
荒屋在那里穷凶极恶，积着薄薄红土
是什么挡住我如此温情的视线？
在蚂蚁的必死之路
脸上盖着树叶的人走来
向日葵被割掉头颅，粗糙糜烂的脖子
伸在天空下如同一排谎言
蓑衣装扮成神，夜里将作恶多端

寒食节出现的呼喊
村里人因抚慰死者而自我克制
我寻找，总带着未遂的笑容
内心伤口与他们的肉眼连成一线
怎样才能进入静安庄
尽管每天都有溺婴尸体和服毒的新娘

They've come back, and the flowers line up in formation, ready to resist

Suddenly, the sounds of childbirth grow louder

I feel the setting sun implode

I wonder: how can I ever be part of

This village where even the birds are silent

Translated by Andrea Lingenfelter

他们回来了，花朵列成纵队反抗
分娩的声音突然提高
感觉落日从里面崩溃
我在想：怎样才能进入
这时鸦雀无声的村庄

THE FIFTH MONTH

This is a day full of suspicion, she has arrived at this place
And the moon reveals its savage light, seeding heartrending secrets

Walking in the dark, the phosporescent night, natural and unadorned
She made the whiteness well-defined
So many nights, one after another, her hands
On your chest keep their mystery
Broadbean flowers are eating up Tranquil Village with great care
Falling asleep is incomparably sweet for others

Along the river, a strange tree sneering faintly
Someone sighs at anonymity, but she doesn't mind
Entering your living body
Gives certain things a shape; are they alive?
A suffering tree alters its appearance overnight
The scarecrow guarding the wheat fields is startled
His roots have disappeared beneath the heaving earth

第五月

这是一个充满怀疑的日子，她来到此地
月亮露出凶光，繁殖令人心碎的秘密

走在黑暗中，夜光磷磷，天然无饰
她使白色变得如此分明
许多夜晚重新换过，她的手
放在你胸前依然神秘
蚕豆花细心地把静安庄吃掉
他人的入睡芬芳无比

在水一方，有很怪的树轻轻冷笑
有人叹息无名，她并不介意
进入你活生生的身体
使某些东西成形，它们是活的?
痛苦的树在一夜间改变模样
麦田守望人惊异
波动的土地使自己的根彻底消失

She goes, she returns, with a dream-like quality

At the corner of two low walls

A gigantic pomegranate

Displays its lusty colors

Walking languidly, despising all the winds

With a hand in all kinds of evil, she's always been like this

The tender and intimate voice in your heart

Grew faint long ago

For the other insomniacs, in the fifth month, recalling

Planchette and incantations spread an unconscious fear

Translated by Andrea Lingenfelter

她去，她来，带着虚幻的风度
硕大无朋的石榴
从拐角两边的矮墙
露出内在淫欲的颜色
缓缓走动，憎恨所有的风
参与各种事物的恶毒，她一向如此
早已变成不明之物
甘美倾心的声音在你心内
其他失眠者的五月，因想到
扶乩的咒语，微微泛起不自觉的怯意

THE TWELFTH MONTH

The time has come for me to leave Tranquil Village
The mare still stamps her black hooves
The northwest wind blows across this no-man's land
Reminding the herd of calves of war...

At this point there's no way to confirm the shape of emptiness
The setting sun descends like pestilence, sitting over the village
My heart wounded like a tree,
My hands arranging the desire of white sap. Awakened by your calls

I look up and see a flying saucer, it appears out of nowhere
Furtively caresses the stone in my breast, kisses me good-bye
The whole village has put up with your moodiness,
Shoes filled with grains of sand, the air thick with the scent of wheat
    grass

The sun is high and cold
Wishing with all its heart it could become a sentient being
An old woman flips over a fish that's in agony
In every corner, human skulls full of dust
Parched smiles on their faces, trembling shadows

第十二月

如今已到离开静安庄的时候
牝马依然敲响它的黑蹄
西北风吹过无人之境
使一群牛犊想起战争……

迄今无法证明空虚的形体
落日像瘟疫降临，坐在村头
内心疮痍如一棵树
双手布置白色树液的欲望，被你唤醒

我抬头看见飞碟，偶然出现
偷偷抚摸怀中之石，临别与我接吻
整个村庄蒙受你的阴沉
鞋子装满沙粒，空气密布麦芽气味

太阳又高又冷
努力想成为有脑髓的生物
年迈的妇女翻动痛苦的鱼
每个角落，人头骷髅装满尘土
脸上露出干燥的微笑，晃动的黑影

The sound of footsteps come from underground, flowing like blood

Butterflies see how they look in their flight from death

Like you, distance lies at the center of everything

Here on this ground, I'm still in a strange land

All along in this village where even the sparrows are silent

I've heard the ancient guttural sound born in this moment

Ribs secretly aching

An interval of approachable time opens for me the immense gate of night

A girl is standing in the dusk

Gray horse, gray human shadows

Flagstones illuminated by kicked up sparks

Nausea, like rain pattering on the rooftop

The depressing birthing of a baby

We are leaving

Taking with us our unfathomable flesh and blood

In the end you could say I came here

Eager to please,

Now I'm leaving, my good will spent

Smoke brings tears to my eyes, my gaze turns inward

Dispirited bits of samsara and ancient wrinkles

步行的声音来自地底，如血液流动
蝴蝶们看见自己投奔死亡的模样
与你相似，距离是所有事物的中心
在地面上，我仍是异乡的孤身人

始终在这个鸦雀无声的村庄
耳听此时出生的古老喉音
肋骨隐隐作痛
一度可接近的时间为我打开黑夜的大门

女孩子站在暮色里
灰色马、灰色人影
石板被踢起的火花照亮
一种恶心感觉像雨淋在屋顶
婴儿的苦闷产生
我们离开
带着无法揣测的血肉之躯

归根结蒂，我到过这里
讨人喜欢
我走的时候却不怀好意
被烟熏出眼泪，目光朝向
伤了元气的轮回部分和古老的皱纹

Low-flying birds bore through my heart and leave me empty
The old elm with my birth date carved into it
Bound once more with hemp ropes as old as my father
Is prideful because it gave us life

The villagers stand on the south-facing slope
Suspicious of daytime, taking the long way around again, back to
    their evening rest
The elders' profound gazes send winter's malice into retreat

Leaving cracks in my strong face.
The first thing I saw was a magical child standing beneath a tree
He's wondering still
How all of this came to be
During these unseen moments

Translated by Andrea Lingenfelter

低飞的鸟穿过内心使我一无所剩
刻着我出生日期的老榆树
又结满我父亲年龄的旧草绳
因给予我们生命而骄傲

村里的人站在向阳的斜坡上
对白昼怀疑，又绕尽远路回到夜里休息
老年人深深的目光使布满恶意的冬天撤退

使我强有力的脸上出现裂痕
最先看见魔术的孩子站在树下
他仍在思索
所有一切是怎样变出来的
在那些看不见的时刻

FACING A PHONE CALL

I spend a whole day   coping with my fear
Every day I'm alarmed   beneath the whole world's sky
I want to splash some of life's speech   in every direction

Grass bends   because it fears wind
Bullets fall   because they fear targets
Phones ring   because they
insist on the right to speak

Okay, the tongue will jump up
to welcome another dance
to forecast conditions at work   changes in climate
the progress of war and   illness

Many people
all following the same line
disappear   Many other people
following the same line
come crawling over

去面对一个电话

花一整天　我在应付我的害怕
每天我都在全世界的天空下
惶惑　生命中的若干言语
我要去洒向四面八方

草弯下　是因为怕风
子弹落下　是因为害怕目标
电话响了　是因为它
坚持说话的权利

好吧，舌头要跳起来
迎接再一次的舞蹈
要预测工作情况　气候变化
还要预测情绪波动
战争走向和　疾病

许多人
都沿着一条线
不见了　又有许多人
沿着一条线
爬过来

This has been called the age of the greatest decline

Complete decline   will bring about

the most moving changes

It's all right, there's a guy who loves me

and shares my life with me

He's not a hopeless wreck

He's not built from crumbling bits of scrap

He's not even the one I'd like to be infatuated with me

It seems we're approaching

the essence of love

We'll be like some animals

swallowing each other   A great bank of clouds will

lift us and carry us away

This should be such a carefree matter

When I face a phone call

I'm weighted down again

Translated by Jami Proctor Xu

这是被称为最衰的时代
衰透了　就有
最动人的变化

还好吧，有一个男人爱我
与我分享生活
他不是绝望者
他也不是豆腐渣工程
他甚至不是我钟意的痴情者

看来我们已经接近
爱的本质
我们就要像某些动物般
互相吞吃　大片的云就要
托起我们奔跑

这原本是多么轻松的事
当我去面对一个电话
我又开始变得沉重

1999

MY BAT

Bat is my secret friend   the clothes I wear

The hair trailing behind me

The reason I go incognito

Abiding with me through endless winters

He's a notably devoted domestic animal

A fragile and empty heart is easiest to touch

A spirit that knows no limits

Nights suspended in the air   embrace his sleep

Bat serves us   no one is aware

Our point of origin is in the world's unfathomable depths

His eccentricity only confirms

His inborn superiority   When early morning shines into our dwelling

He slips away

At first I took him for some sort of wise bird

His zealous digits righting old wrongs

He explains   he broadcasts

Significant distinctions

我的蝙蝠

蝙蝠是我的密友　是我的衣服
是我的头发追随我
隐姓埋名的缘由
漫长的冬天与我同住

他是畜类中最钟情的一种
空虚易碎的心最能打动
茫茫无边的鬼魂
悬空的夜晚　有他的睡眠

蝙蝠是人的伙计　无人知晓
深不可测的世界有我们全面的出发点
他古怪的脾气向来就强调
先天优势　当清晨照射我们的住处
他偷偷离去
起先我以为他是懂事的飞禽
他激情的十指纠正错误
他解释　又公布
那理所当然的区分

Bat is my shadow

His mind tracks me

Gathering reliable intelligence   until

Blind love brings him back to his senses

Lonely wayfarer

His perseverant flight will never match a bird's

For his look of inborn suffering is hard to escape

On sleepless nights   he hangs upside down

Opposing me   deepening the surrounding darkness

Bat is an ancient story

The final sequence of a dream

A bird with strange camouflage

Such a lofty spirit can hardly come to earth

His weighty   carnal form

Has been linked to me from the start

The intimacy of our childhood

Remains unbroken even today

Translated by Andrea Lingenfelter

蝙蝠是我的影子
他的思想跟踪我
获取确切的情报　直至
盲目的爱情使他神智恢复
孤零零的流浪
他执意的飞行永远无法接近鸟类
因他生就的苦难相难以自由
睡不着的夜里　他倒挂着
与我作对　加强四周的黑暗

蝙蝠是古老的故事
是梦中最后的发现
是一个畸形的伪装的鸟
高贵的心难以着陆
他重大的　肉感的形态
始终与我有关
这一切幼时多么熟悉
现在也依然存在

DOLL

When I'm sick of black night

I sit up from dreaming, open my mouth to speak.

The little doll glitters in brown light,

and I speak   in a voice not my own,

muttering the nonsense I've always wanted to say.

Like a still life, like a dark lightbulb

the ugly doll's unhurried,

can't guess its wild heart.

When I twist the lamp switch, dreams ignite the paper,

sad dreams of childhood playmates.

Lying in my hand, one stitch and another

sews its face on, its smile.

I dream of the night   when it opens its mouth to speak

and comes to my bed,

the white bed   dividing life from death,

draped in the white mosquito net.

The doll's eyes

utterly serene,

its doll dream

drifting toward my world;

how bitter my own dreams, seeing you

every night standing at my bedside,

your hands like scissors

whenever you want to hurt me.

Translated by Diana Shi & George O'Connell

玩偶

当我厌倦了黑夜
常常从梦里坐起　开口说话
小小的玩偶闪着褐光
我说话　带着一种不真切的口吻
我说着一直想说的胡言乱语

像静物　也像黑暗中的灯泡
面目丑陋的玩偶不慌不忙
无法识别它内心的狂野
当我拧亮台灯　梦在纸上燃烧
我的梦多么心酸　思念我儿时的玩伴
躺在我手上，一针又一针
我缝着它的面孔和笑容

梦见未来的一夜　它开口说话
来到我的床边
白色的床　分开阴阳两界
白色的蚊帐　是这玩偶的衣裳

这玩偶的眼睛
比万物安宁
这玩偶的梦
飘向我的世界
我的梦多么心酸
夜夜梦见你站在床前
你的手像一把剪刀
时时要把我伤害？

FOURTEEN PLAINSONGS

— FOR MY MOTHER

1 Insomniac Song

On a sleepless night

on so many sleepless nights I hear my restless mother

busy at the stove in the next room washing clothes before dawn

In the dark thinking of the past

its immense bulk   its unmeasurable significance: it stares into the future

That's our secret

an unwritten rule

When we can't sleep   the pulse of the black night

is the rhythm of the song we share

It stares into the future

Thinking of the past blindly

I spend the night imagining

my mother's beautiful young face:

her white cheeks

her long and narrow eyes

float up from the yellowed album

The passions of that era

her expression as keen as an eagle's

She was married   in military uniform my skinny father   at her side

十四首素歌

——致母亲

1. 失眠之歌

在一个失眠的夜晚
在许多个失眠的夜晚
我听见失眠的母亲
在隔壁灶旁忙碌
在天亮前浆洗衣物

盲目地在黑暗中回忆过去
它庞大的体积　它不可捉摸的
意义：它凝视将来

那是我们的秘密
不成文的律条
在失眠时　黑夜的心跳
成为我们之间的歌唱：
它凝视将来

盲目地回忆过去
整整一夜我都在猜想
母亲当年的美貌：
她洁白的双颊
纤细的长眼形
从泛黄的相簿里浮起
还有时代的热血
鹰一样锐利的表情
就这样　她戎装成婚

On sleepless nights   mother moves around the stove

arranging the family's life

does she remember that North China spindle -

her childhood playmate?

Immutable forces make it spin

like the revolutions of constellations

forever circling the hub of a life

For years I've had insomnia

my sleeplessness spinning around a hub:

I stare at my mother

2

Head bowed, I listen deep underground

bones are talking with other bones

glittering eyes dart around

like the spirits of the soil

listening to daylight

from any dark place:

a rooster pecking at grain   as if it were alone

3 Yellow River Ballad

Mother says: "On the banks of the Yellow River

south of the Bend, by a plot of newly planted wheat,

at the end of the road, is our village"

On the south side of the Yellow River is Xie Village

My mother's family name was Xie   her given name hui

身边　站着瘦削的父亲
在失眠之夜　母亲灶前灶后
布置一家的生活场景
她是否回忆起那北方的纺锤——
她童年的玩伴？
永远不变的事物使它旋转
就像群星的旋转
它总要围绕一个生命的轴点

多年来我不断失眠
我的失眠总围绕一个轴点：
我凝视母亲

2

低头听见：地底深处
骨头与骨头的交谈
还有闪烁的眼睛奔忙
就如泥土的灵魂
在任何一种黑暗中
听见白昼时：
雄鸡频频啄食　旁若无人

3. 黄河谣

母亲说："在那黄河边上
在河湾以南，在新种的小麦地旁
在路的尽端，是我们村"

在黄河岸边　是谢庄
母亲姓谢　名讳

Like an ancient hero pure of heart
she walked down from the ridge

The river is broad
its banks forever collapsing   and mud
washes up on the opposite shore
Mother says: "Our land was disappearing"

So people clashed, or moved away
There was looting on moonless nights
One ghost swam across the river
and countless others were filled with wild hopes
The girls were blossoming
but their lovers were dead
"The freezing winds that blow back and forth across the Yellow River
stream over their young bones"

Though the river ran the ochre of drought, and the shingled shoreline
    was rugged
my mother was stunningly beautiful
her face like an apricot
rosy as peach blossoms
When she strode along the ridge
she was the prettiest girl by the Yellow River
When she walked barefoot on its banks, stepping on the washing
the young men felt an icy stab
and shuddered with regret

若香草和美人之称
她从坡脊走来

河流扩大
坡地不断坍塌　　泥土
涌到对面的河滩之上
母亲说："我们的地在一点点失去"

于是就有了械斗、迁徙
就有了月黑风高时的抢劫
一个鬼魂的泅渡
就有了无数鬼魂的奢望
那些韶华红颜的年轻女孩
他们的爱人都已逝去
"在黄河上刮来的刮去的寒风
每年刮着他们年轻的尸骨"

虽然河水枯黄、石滩粗糙
但母亲出落得动人
她的脸像杏子
血色像桃花
当她走过坡脊
她是黄河边上最可爱的事物
当她在河边赤脚踩踏衣服
一股寒意刺痛了岸边的小伙
使他们的内心一阵阵懊恼

My forty years went by more quickly than my mother's
one by one, they flew away like birds
Year after year, time passed by, unremarkable
an inborn sadness locked inside my marrow
and those who walked beside me never noticed
My forty years went by more quickly than my mother's

"What kind of man is our future?
What kind of man makes us wait till the twilight of our years?
What kind of man makes getting him
as painful as losing him?
What kind of man
will lie beside us in sleep and death?"

My mother walks along the ridge
book bag under her arm   She still hasn't learned the ways of
a love worth keeping till the end of her days
She already knows the pitfalls of being a woman
and the shameful things that go with love
She has no silks   she's dressed in hemp
Whoever sees her
will lose himself completely

我的四十岁比母亲来得更早
像鸟儿一只只飞走
那一年年熟视无睹的时间
我天生的忧伤锁在骨髓里
不被走在我身旁的人所察觉
我的四十岁比母亲来得更早

　"什么样的男人是我们的将来？
什么样的男人使我们等到迟暮？
什么样的男人在我们得到时
与失去一样悲痛？
什么样的男人
与我们的睡眠和死亡为伴？"

我的母亲从坡脊上走来
挟着书包　还没有学会
一种适合她终身的爱　但
已经知道作女人的弊病
和恋爱中那些可耻的事情
她没有丝绸　身着麻布衣衫
谁看见她
谁就会忘记自己的一切

Turning faraway events into tragedies

making beauty everlasting

the brush of time glides rapidly along

giving birth to words   like pebbles pouring down

rapidly sliding banks

careless of the suffering dead in fresh graves

Flowing east   flowing south

slapping the opposite shore

careless of the people who died for it on either side

4

Everything withers in the end

Time has the upper hand   when giving out alms

to sustain the flesh

Semen flows from every cavity

right until the last drop at the hour of death

5 The Song of Being Eighteen

Mother said: when she was young

Strife and turmoil found her

A rifle in her hands

corpse-covered fields filling her vision

My mother: leader of a children's brigade

Her commander rode on horseback, shouldering a gun

a man renowned for his courage

Life and death

were like boudoir games   she said

She set aside her shuttle

and followed her lover far away

使遥远的事物变得悲哀
使美变得不朽
时间的笔在急速滑动
产生字　就像那急速滑落的河滩上
倾泄如注的卵
不顾及新坟中死亡者的痛苦
流到东　流到南
又拍打到对面
不顾及人们为它死在两岸

4

事物都会凋零
时间是高手　将其施舍
充作血肉的营养
精液流出它们自己的空间
包括临终时最后的一点

5. 十八岁之歌

母亲说：在她的少女时代
风暴和斗争来到她的身边
钢枪牵起了她的手
尸骸遍野塞满了她的眼睛

我的母亲：儿童团长
她的兄长挎枪乘马
是远近驰名的勇士
生生死死
不过如闺房中的游戏　她说
她放下织梭
跟着爱人远去

The enemy arrived pointing guns and firing cannons

The village was in chaos   kinsmen scattered to the four winds

In mother's eyes I saw

images of these people:

cousins and aunts

a branch of my bloodline

I turn to a lifeless face in the album

Some stare out sternly

some are tight-lipped and glum

Warfare, sacrifice, unwavering dedication

their purity drenched in blood

blazed like fire   through years of war

My eighteenth year brought nothing of note

My eighteenth year bore no flowers

Beautiful as the sky   and yet

every sheaf of nerves in my body

could feel plants withering clump by clump

Birds dying one by one   The riot of flowers

inside my body exploded under cover of darkness

crashing into the dry bones that surround them

My eighteenth year brought nothing of note

In those years of war   my mother

threaded through the space between the instants

of life and death   Her fair features and

rosy cheeks colored

the strangest gambit of the war

敌人来到：携枪，或运炮
村庄被倾覆　亲戚四散奔逃
在母亲的眼里　我看到
那些人的影像：
他们是我的姑表中亲
血缘里的一部分
有时从相册里探出没有呼吸的脸
或者目光严峻
或者沉默寡言
战斗、献身、矢志不移
他们被血浸透的单纯
像火一样点燃　在那些战争年代

我的十八岁无关紧要
我的十八岁开不出花来
与天空比美　但
我的身体里一束束的神经
能感觉到植物一批批落下

鸟儿在一只只死去　我身内的
各种花朵在黑夜里左冲右突
撞在前前后后的枯骨上
我的十八岁无关紧要

在那些战争年代　我的母亲
每天在生的瞬间和死的瞬间中
穿行　她的美貌和
她双颊的桃花点染出
战争最诡奇的图案

She cut off her glossy hair   striding purposefully

eluding guns in the woods and

fuses held in the enemy's hands   and then

she hurled her body full tilt

towards yet another blast

All the stories mother told

had rousing conclusions

and extraordinary deaths — sacrifice or

an abstract and even sadder impulse unlike me with my fretting about

    death

my anxiousness about this false and empty world

and my long present   but soon to depart

misgivings about going home

No one comes to hear our speeches

No one cares that we're here

Of course no one is chasing us down

in a world of mortal prospects   What's more

no bullets are whistling past

our ears   I don't have five stars

to pin in my hair   I've merely

let my body be shot through with illusions

and allowed a twist of fate to become

the ideology in my bones

她秀发剪短　步履矫健
躲避着丛林中的枪子和
敌人手中的导火线　然后
她积极的身躯跑向
另一个爆破点

母亲讲述的故事
都有大胆的结论
不寻常的死亡方式——牺牲
或不具体的
更悲切的动机　不同于我
对死亡的担心
对虚无世界的忧心忡忡
对已经到来　将要离去的
归宿的疑问

没有人来听我们的演说
也没有人关心我们相互的存在
当然　也没有人来追捕我们
亡命的生涯　而且
也没有子弹穿过
我们的鬓发　没有五星
成为我的发饰　我只是
让幻想穿透我的身体
让一个命运的逆转成为我
骨髓里的思想

6

— "In the end, we couldn't bear it"

A dark-eyed woman sitting tall beside the fire

She'd charged forward with her unisex haircut

Separation like a knife poised

A man's heart slides into its sheath

But a woman holds it tight until she bleeds

7 The Song of Reconstruction

My birthplace:

a temple   a few crumbling rooms

high up in a black pagoda

My protector: a local girl

War had wreaked havoc on many mothers' labors

Fetuses looked out on the world like ghosts   and yet

we lacked the power to choose our time

Had there been a choice

I would have been the first born

rather than the last   and if

choice could alter a human being's first step

I could have evaded all manner of fates

whether one of the best

or an early death

In reality   I was born

with a stubborn streak

Would I fail to perceive what was best:

staying inside the cramped darkness of my mother's body

or being out in the expansive daylight of the world?

6

—— "最终，我们无法忍受"
黑眼女子端坐火边
中立的发型前趋
离别像一把刀　等待
男人的心入鞘
而女人掌握了使它流血的技巧

7. 建设之歌

我的出生地：
一座寺庙　几间危房
高处一座黑塔
护卫我的：一个本地女孩
战争搞乱了母亲们的生育
胎儿如幽灵向外张望　但
没有权利选择时间
如果能够选择
我该会选择第一个出生
而不是最后　如果
选择能够改变人类的第一步
我将躲开各种各样的命运
或者最好的一种
或者早夭

事实上　我出生：
向着任意的方向
来不及分析哪样更好？
在母体的小小黑暗里
还是在世界广大的白昼中

All of creation rushes in like a river
stabbing my eyes like sunlight
For several months in a row   I've kept my eyes shut tight
lying on my bed   That's where I'll be
lying 'til the end of my days

My mother   in uniform
red flags and songs, a rising tide,
adorned her
but I   would wait for years
for another ecstatic era
copying my mother's way of dressing
as if I were going to a costume party

"We were founders"   Mother said
Her ideals seemed more important
than life itself   Founding is joyful
compared with destruction
That's something anyone can understand

.

Hammers strike blueprints
A modern city in the high pitch of reconstruction
grows up around us
Immense, imposing, and who will spare a thought for
the historic city lying prostrate at its feet
That's the beauty of conflict

万物像江河奔来
像阳光刺痛我的双眼
接连几个月　我紧闭两眼
躺在床上　那是我
终身要躺的地方

我的母亲　戎装在身
红旗和歌潮如海地
为她添妆
而我　则要等到多年后
在另一个狂欢的时代
模仿母亲的着装
好似去参加一个化装舞会

"我们是创建者"　母亲说
她的理想似乎比生命本身
更重要　创建是快乐的
比之于毁坏
人们懂得这一点

铁锤敲击蓝图
现代之城在建设的高音区
普遍地成长
高大、雄伟，有谁在乎
匍匐在它脚下的时间之城
那有争议的美

Mother busy with nation-building
her sensual beauty rubbed away bit
by bit and an even more profound place in time
reveals an immutable power

8

Not one man looks back
They crawl out of the needle's eye
staring down the enemy
Engaging in dignified sex
until they're laid to rest in the wintry cold

9 The Song of the Girl Who Observes the Ants

Ants are milling around   shuttling back and forth
as if moving a chaste afternoon
one after another   lined up single file
sometimes embracing

"I heard you talking among yourselves"
the girl who observes the ants   I say

She appeared   surrounded by such minuteness
She was that large   genuinely large
She had a crown of her own
The queen ant had her own kind of style

为建设奔忙的母亲
肉体的美一点点地消散
而时间更深邃的部分
显出它永恒不变的力量

8

没有一个男人回头望
他们爬出针眼
注视敌人的眼睛
在交媾时威风八面
直到在寒冷中下葬

9. 观察蚂蚁的女孩之歌

蚂蚁移动着　来回穿梭
像移动一个纯净的下午
一个接一个　排列成行
偶然相互拥抱

"我听见你们在说话"
观察蚂蚁的女孩　我说

她出现了　在周围极端的小中
她是那样大　真正的大
她有自己的冠冕
蚁王有她自己的风范

"I listened with my entire body

my inner antennae extending their infinite reach

I smelled the wind, the nectared weather

and the speech of a world at peace"

— the girl who observes the ants   "It's me"

Ants overflow my matchbox

living in a world without wind

without speech   When they

gently catch your eye   what is being caught?

From within something invisible

we gather invisible news

And then   I'm suddenly inside

a gigantic matchbox   That giant

crown of hers   covers me without pity

Her enormous breaths and sighs

buffet my fate   My body

her form in a young girl's eyes

and the form of the matchbox in her eyes

embody the mutability of this world

"Mama, please give me a matchbox"

the girl who observes the ants   I say

"我用整个的身体倾听
内心的天线在无限伸展
我嗅到风、蜜糖天气
和一个静态世界里的话语"
——观察蚂蚁的女孩　"是我"
蚂蚁溢满了我的火柴盒
它所在的世界没有风
没有话语　它们
轻轻一触目　触摸到什么？
从那不可见的事物中
得到我们不可见的消息

这时　我突然置身在
那巨大的火柴盒里　她那
巨大的冠冕　残忍地盖住我
她那巨大的呼吸和叹气
吹动我的命运　我的身体
她在一个女孩眼中的形体
和火柴盒在她眼中的形体
是这个世界的变异

"妈妈，请给我一个火柴盒"
观察蚂蚁的女孩　我说

Freed from care and released from woe

— an old man bends over a game of Go

regulates his breathing thinking neither of the past nor hereafter

memories rise sudden as whirlwinds

his withered and boney fingers grown sharper with age

11 The Song of the Dancing Woman

Mother said: I named you "Ping," rootless duckweed

where do you wander? Duckweed, drifting on the water

I can't conjure a smile in that mysterious mirror

I, the next generation of my family

had a cold and lonely childhood

a difficult adolescence

Now I'm entering an age of solitude

My thirtieth year was just so-so

Feelings that once seduced me no longer matter

"When love comes calling, turn your eyes away"

At the table: a cup of bad coffee

An afternoon of whispering and touching

A love we called Platonic

destroyed my youth

10

一切都无忧无虑
——老人低头弈棋
调整呼吸　不考虑生前身后
急如旋风的纪念
他的枯干骨指老而益尖

11. 舞蹈的女人之歌

母亲说：你本名萍
萍踪何处？　萍影漂泊
神秘的镜子里我笑不出

我、家族的下一代
经过一个肃杀的童年
和一个苦恼的少年
现在进入寂寞的时代
我的三十岁马马虎虎

诱惑我的感情已不重要
"当爱来临，将取走你的眼睛"
桌边：一杯劣质咖啡
一下午的偎颈共语
一个被称为柏拉图式的爱情
毁了我的青春

My mother couldn't believe what she saw
not to mention the white-haired elders:
In the moonlight   by the riverbank
my body shaking all over   like a she-monster spewing fire
I began a ghoulish dance   bones making a horrible sound
My form swaying there for all to see
filled her with loathing

My body blazed before them
left them glassy-eyed and dumbstruck
unable to comprehend how
the beauty of the flesh could shudder
along with the shame of the flesh
accustomed as they were to self-sacrifice
and zealous melodies

And so   the dance is flung from the center
carrying mother's rebuke to the ends of the earth
There are people like me who don't see things as they are
The wind   takes each one's miseries far far away
My twentieth year was just so-so

I've been drifting so long   toiling for years
am madly in love with yet another man
At last I've made my peace   with youth
with a dance that won't be cruel again

我的母亲不相信她的亲眼所见
还有那些白发长者：
在月光下　在临水的河边
我全身抽搐　如吐火女怪
鬼似的起舞　骨骼发出吓人的声响
我当众摇摆的形体
使她憎恶

我就地燃烧的身体
让他们目瞪口呆
他们不明白为什么
肉体的美会如此颤抖
连同肉体的羞耻
他们习惯于那献身的
信仰的旋律

于是　舞蹈从中心散尽
带着母亲的斥责四处逃掉
还有我那些不明真相的同类
风　把他们各自的骚乱送得很远
我的二十岁马马虎虎

如今漂泊日久　劳作多年
与另一名男子爱欲如狂
我终于到达一个和谐　与青春
与一个不再残酷的舞蹈

And so in one night

pressed by beauty

beneath a winding tendril of hair

love and hate change their tunes

fostering an illusion

trying to keep up with the elixir of youth

crying out in pain or melting with joy

13 The Song of Black and White Paragraphs

Now   I strike my black and white

keyboard

pleased with myself

pleased with myself though it might seem stupid

Can't I think for myself anymore?

A bunch of letters of the alphabet

Big Five text?

Like marsh grasses   waving in a blue expanse

can they flow from the original face of things

not knowing the first stage of decoding

they appear: the final look of things

My fortieth year arrived more quickly than my mother's

The wounds in my marrow were of her making

She didn't know   but still her thinking

spread through my body in secret   the way

the scent of peaches in a bowl subtly

12

因此在一夜间
被美逼近
在一绺发丝缠绕下
爱和恨　改弦易辙
培育出幻影
恸哭或销魂

13. 黑白的片断之歌

现在　我敲打我那黑白的
打字机键盘
颇为自得
像干一件蠢事般自得

我已不再用自己的心灵思索?
那一大堆字母
组合成的五笔字形？
像水草　在一片蓝色中流动
能否流出事物的本来面目
它不知道一级解码的过程
它呈现：就是终极的面目

我的四十岁比母亲来得早
骨髓里的忧伤是她造成的
她不知道　但她的思想
暗暗散发进我的体内　就像
一盘桃子的芳香暗暗

fans out and enters my nose   She left

the most profound mark on my exhausted existence

deeper and wider than any black and white letters

My fortieth year arrived more quickly than my mother's

While I strike my black and white

keyboard   elbows pressed to my desk

Mother sits over her sewing machine

elbows propping up her frailty

striking her ever simplifying life

From her gesture

to my gesture

one thing has never changed:

that desolate and final

pure gesture

not the projection of an idea

There's a tiny blood vessel in me

a dense little spot

that came from my mother's face

a peach-like rosy pigment

I couldn't inherit

the regret that became a part of life

散发进我的鼻孔　她造成
我倦怠生命中最深远的痕迹
比任何黑白字母的渗透更有力
我的四十岁比母亲来得更早

当我敲打我那黑白的
打字机键盘　用肘紧靠桌面
母亲弯腰坐在她的缝纫机旁
用肘支撑衰老
敲打她越来越简单的生活
从她的姿势
到我的姿势
有一点从未改变：
那凄凉的、最终的
纯粹的姿势
不是以理念为投影
在我体内有一点血脉
稠密的一点
来自母亲的容颜
她那桃花式的血色素
我未能继承
成为生命里部分的遗憾

Other than that   I did inherit:

flesh and blood from the Yellow River's banks

bones from ten miles of barren strands

dust from the water's edge

days from above the clouds

my build from the male side and

my temperament from the female

Reaching the age of forty

old and worn   it piles up:

the final look of things

Beginning with those collapsing banks

a village's mounting ambitions

the mud shifting elsewhere bit by bit

In the end, an immutable mutability

gradually nears the essence of time

where our elbows are firmly braced

14

So when we speak of poetry   we no longer waver:

— it's like stirring ice cubes

it's like pairs of cymbals crashing into each other's faces

Wounded suffering like glass—

Words, fair faces, and love at an impasse

Translated by Andrea Lingenfelter

除此之外　我继承着：
黄河岸边的血肉
十里枯滩的骨头
水边的尘沙
云上的日子
来自男方的模子和
来自女方的脾性
还有那四十岁就已来到的
衰老　它重叠：
就是终极的面目

始于那坍塌的坡地
和一点点移向他方的泥土
堆积起来的村庄的意志
终于一种不变的变化
缓慢地，靠近时间本质
在我们双肘确立的地方

14

于是谈到诗　不再动摇：
——就如推动冰块
在酒杯四壁赤脚跳跃
就如铙钹撞击它自己的两面
伤害　玻璃般的痛苦——
词、花容，和走投无路的爱

A GAME

Two lines   one river
B and S   L and F
They're all ready

They all hate and fear
that guy   But he's going to
cross the river   He constantly
wants to wade across, wants to dive under, wants to take flight
None of the four beauties can help him

Guy D   go deeply love the object of your desire
If you have B
you'll lose S   If
you have F   you can have L
If you love L   you must offer up
your B

一个游戏

两根线　一条河
B 和 S　L 和 F
它们都已就绪

它们都对那个男人
又恨又怕　但是他就要
过河了　他不停地
想蹚，想潜，和想飞
四个美人都帮不了他

男人 D　去深爱你渴望的事物吧
如果你拥有 B
你就失去了 S　　如果
你有了 F　你也可以有 L
如果你爱 L　你必须贡献
你的 B

There are several more women than men

Of course the man is perched atop a lofty divan

He isn't moved by women's sexual love

He isn't moved by women's tenderness

He isn't moved by women's sacrifices

The women become restless and anxious   Their

spirits   have been pricked by pins into specimens

None of the four beauties can help him

B and S   L and F

They are about to form one line

They are D's horizon

They surround him   They screech in unison

He constantly   kills their IQs

Within entanglements the world

      completes its dualism

Also within entanglements   men and women

      complete their retribution

Translated by Jami Proctor Xu

女人比男人多出几个
男人当然高枕无忧
他也不为她们的性爱所动
他也不为她们的温柔所动
他也不为她们的牺牲所动

她们开始焦燥   她们的
灵魂   已被大头针扎为标本
四个美人也帮不了他

B 和 S   L 和 F
它们就要合成一根线
它们就是 D 的地平线
她们围住他   齐声尖叫
他也不停地   杀她们的智商

世界就在纠缠里
　　完成它的二元论
男人和女人   也在纠缠里
　　完成他们的报应

1999.8.16

HYPNOSIS

She tells me   your entire life
is locked inside
your sleep

Her gestures   her tone of voice
and the life of all the world
bestow on me
a moment of profound exhaustion

The sweetness of her breath   insinuates
itself into my pineal gland
as sleep overtakes me
I see a butterfly from a previous existence

Going back   yet unable
the first half of my life
struggles desperately in my sleep   she discovers
my spirit
has dosed itself   with millennial melatonin

Translated by Andrea Lingenfelter

催眠术

她告诉我　人的一生
都密封在
自己的睡眠里

她的手势　她的语气
还有全世界的一生
都提供给我
一分钟的深深倦意

她吐气如兰　向
大脑中的松果腺体
我昏昏欲睡时
看到了前世的蝴蝶

回去　回不去
我的前半辈子
在睡眠中厮杀　她发现
我的灵魂
服用了　世纪末的褪黑素

SCISSORHANDS' DIALOGUE
FOR FRIDA KAHLO

1

"Tell me about it, the rigid escape"
A vein and many branches and leaves aflutter
Encircling viscera   swaying by instinct

"Tell me, but be patient"
Long-bladed shears offered up to Kahlo
Bring infection to my lungs

A butterfly beats its wings   igniting the rosy red of her lips
Women's colors come from pain
Convulsions and rage

"Tell me, rigid scissor hands
I can't lie down in the middle of this random pounding
To let that elderly doctor's steel needle
And his diagnostic gaze
Primp and dress me up like that"

"Pulverized vertebrae, I opted for an iron rod,
I got the cure I needed"

剪刀手的对话

献给弗里达 · 卡罗

一

"对我说吧，僵硬的逃亡"
一根脉络和无数枝叶移动
围绕肝脏　本能地摇摆

"对我说吧，耐心点"
献给卡罗的长形剪刀
导致我肺部的感染

蝴蝶一扑　点燃她满嘴的桃红
女人的颜色来自痛
痉挛，和狂怒

"对我说吧，僵硬的剪刀手
我不会躺在七零八落的敲打中
让那年迈医生的钢针
和他考察病理的目光
为我如此妆扮"

"捣碎的脊柱，不如一根铁钉
我已得到足够的治疗"

2

I lean over the glass   a razor's edge

Examining my pores

And this damaged bag of bones

Me, roaming among the colors of the rainbow

Entering the depths... surfacing in the shallows

"Women will always go to great lengths for beauty"

Look at the iron rod inside my body

Beneath a bloom of sad and angry flames

How were those rainbow hues transformed into the patterns

    carved on her breast

In the basin bloody water

Ripples with lipstick colors

Icy destiny

Me, the dizzy hawker

Spewing waterfalls

Scorning the contagion with red and swollen eyes

"Glass and diamonds

Both catch the eye with their allure

Spurring women to madness"

二

俯身向玻璃　剃刀边缘
察看毛孔的健康状况
和受伤的皮囊
我，游离在五光十色之间
深入……浅出……
"为了美，女人永远着忙"

请看体内的锻铁钉
在一朵忧郁烈焰的炙烤下
斑斓　怎样变成她胸前的雕花图案

洗涤槽中，血水
与口红的色彩波动
冰冷的上方
我那眩晕的兜售者
从红肿的双眼里
喷出瀑布　蔑视感染

"玻璃或钻石
还有撩拨人的目光
促使她们疯狂"

3

Hummingbird, embraced by thorny vines
Brushing past her fevered
Bleeding neck   creating a beautiful face

Butterfly beats its wings   flutters up
From Kahlo's ice-cold metal bed
Flashing, golden
Four wheels creaking
Witness to this woman's battlefield

Each and every living hair and
Her heavy eyebrows
Are the fertile climate of her heart
Piercing the plaster cast
Piercing the collapsing sky

"I have grasped the shape of terror"
Kahlo leans forward, whispering
I hear the scissors slicing
Plaster, and cane
They're broken hearted

三

蜂鸟，刺藤的拥抱
掠过她狂热的
流血的脖子　创造美的脸庞

蝴蝶一扑　飞起来
从卡罗冰凉的铁床上
闪光、金黄
吱吱响的四只车轮
目睹了这个女人的战场

一根根向上长的毛发
和她的浓眉是
内心茂盛繁荣的气象
穿透石膏护身褡
穿透塌下来的一片天

"我已掌握了恐惧的形状"
卡罗俯身向前，低声细语
我听见剪刀轧轧之响
以及石膏、拐杖
它们痛断肝肠

4

Razor's edge   flashing diamantine lights
Become a moving pattern on my breast
Hairstyles leave dreamlike memories   now long, now short
The dark night's fragrance washes over my eyes until they gleam

A pair of eyes the closer they get to the glass   the darker they grow
Her vomit strikes spinning beams of light
Making me sad: the other side of joy

The other side: come see
The dense and the thin   the black and white of light and shadow
Plants decreasing from multitudes to just one
She's rinsed clean of color…
Why not pick up a glass

"For beauty, women bleed in secret"

They bleed   but who cares:
The scissors in her heart are cutting
Love's true outlines   she stares
Eyes sharp as an animal's
Two legs scissoring   hissing, hissing

Hissing   as prickly as salt
It's not a moan
It's not easy on the ear
It's the hopeless and tangled pistil of the tongue

四

剃刀边缘　闪着钻石的光
成为我前胸主动的安排
发式在意念中变幻　忽长忽短
暗夜的香味浆洗着双眼

双眼　越靠近玻璃面　越黑
她的呕吐打击着盘旋的光线
令人担忧：欢乐的背面

背面：你来看
浓浓淡淡　黑白的光影
一株植物从最多减到单一
她洗净颜色……
何如一杯在手

"为了美，女人暗暗淌血"

淌血　谁会在乎：
她心中的剪刀正在剪
一个爱的真轮廓　她注视
动物之眼一样犀利
两腿绞动着　发出嘶嘶声

嘶嘶　盐一样刺痛的声音
它不是从口中呜咽
也不是在耳边温柔
它是一根舌头绞动无望的花茎

5

In the darkness   my legs extended
Dancing with Kahlo
"Women: coming and going
Burning away your essence like candles"

"Don't pay attention to what meets the eye
Kahlo, our broken arms
Obey the desiring heart and its urgings"

The young find pleasure in the pretty pieces of glass
Suffering for shattered fragments
While the old subside into silence
Like the spirits of strong and faithful stones
Spellbound, they remain whole within

"For beauty, women will suffer heartbreak"

A pair of legs crossing   scissorhands
Snipping away at shapes in the darkness
Busily chopping, cutting, splitting
Busily disinfecting, glinting
Who could be better at
Wielding this scalpel   and sneering
At our common spinal malady
Kahlo — how can we know if the source of our pain is the scissors' tip
Or the depths of our own marrow?

Translated by Andrea Lingenfelter

五

在黑暗中　我的腿脚伸出
与卡罗跳舞
　"女人们：来，去
蜡烛般烧毁自己的本性"

　"不必管那眼神够得着的搜寻
卡罗，我们破碎的背柱
服从内心性欲的主动"

年幼者取悦漂亮的玻璃
为毁灭的碎片受苦
年长者沉默不语
像坚强有力的石头的灵魂
着魔时，也保持内部的完好无损

　"为了美，女人痛断肝肠"

双腿绞动着　剪刀手
修剪黑暗的形状
忙着切开、砍、分割
忙着消毒、闪光
何人如此适合
握住这把手术刀　挂满嘲笑
要对付我们共同的腰病
卡罗——我们怎样区分来自剪刀刀锋
或是来自骨髓深处的痛？

THE BLIND MASSEUR AND SOME OF HIS METHODS

1

"Relax your hands," the blind man leans over
Kneading the small of my back, as if he were kneading stone
The waist of life is so empty
It hurts

Day after day the blind man massages
Kneading backs that are harder than stone

2

"Be mindful of the climate, climate changes everything,"
Plum blossom needle held in the blind man's hand
I strain to move my head: "What is that?"

Is it life that's fragile
Or is it bones, joints, and bone density?
Plum blossom needles stab my head

3

"Please tap my first vertebra, it's sore"
The blind man's hand plays out a melody on white keys
"Why does it sound so sad?"

盲人按摩师的几种方式

1

"请把手放下"，盲人俯身
推拿腰部，也像推拿石头
生活的腰多么空虚
引起疼痛

盲人一天又一天推拿按摩
推拿比石头还硬的腰部

2

"注意气候，气候改变一切"
梅花针执在盲人之手
我尽力晃动头部："这是什么？"

生命，是易碎的事物
还是骨头，骨节，骨密度？
梅花针扎在我的头部

3

"请敲骨椎第一节，那里疼痛"
盲人的手按下旋律的白键
"这声音怎么这样凄凉？"

I know where the pain comes from
It's the nature of life itself, and nothing to do with this massage
But the massage has reached a state of harmony
The blind man taps, day after day
Sharing in the rhythms of my bones

4

"Turn over, breathe evenly"
The blind man's hands play a melody on black keys

A stormy solo improvisation
His vacant eyes are without complaint or desire
Even his breathing is unusually calm
His hands massage the problems of the world
The blind man works in a blind man's ways

He thinks about the lightness and speed of his touch
As we face the same direction

5

"Pay attention to changes in your sacrum," he says
His fingers know the world's accupressure points by heart
His palms are practiced in Eastern and Western ways

When he applies force, ten fingers press down
The profound strength of his whole body concentrated here and
    knowing
One kind of pain has already been erased

我知道疼痛的原因
是生命的本质，与推拿无关
但推拿已进入和谐的境界
盲人一天又一天敲打
分享我骨头里的节奏

4

"转过身去，调匀呼吸"
盲人的手按下旋律的黑键

暴风雨般的即兴弹奏
他空洞的眼里无怨无欲
甚至他的呼吸也极度平静
他的两手推拿世间的问题
盲人有盲人的方式

他思索下手的轻重缓急
与我们的方向一致

5

"请注意骶骨的变化"，他说
他的手指熟知全世界的穴位
他的手掌兼修中西两种功力

当他使劲，十根指头落下
贯注全身的一股深邃力量知道
一种痛苦已被摧毁

Another kind of pain comes from deep in my heart
From the suitable cut of the white gown
And my tentative pulse

6

The blind man feels his way, day after day
Familiar things, bit by bit
Bit by bit achieving complete clarity

From a rigid piece of stone, or
A dust mote dancing in the air

A man and a woman, both of them blind
Unable to see Life and Death amidst all the changes
Able to see the transformations within Life and Death

7

Once, he takes out a pair of jars
The first of them empty, the other one empty as well

A bead of water oozes slowly from my body
But he can't see it, and then he draws out
The air inside, lights a piece of alcohol-soaked cotton
What is he trying to achieve?

Apart from my fourteen lumbar vertebrae
There are tremors of cold deep in my bones…

另一种痛苦来自肺腑
来自白色袍子的适当切入
以及我那怯懦的心跳

6

盲人一天又一天摸索
熟悉的事物，渐渐地
渐渐地达到澄明的高度

从一块坚硬的石头，或者
在空气中飞舞的跳动的尘埃

一男一女，两个盲人
看不见变易中的生死
看得见生死中的各种变易

7

一次，他拿出两个罐子
其中一个是空的，另一个也空

一滴水就从身体里慢慢溢出
但是他看不见，现在他抽掉
里面的空气，点燃酒精棉
他想要得到什么？

除了腰椎的十四个关节
还有骨头深处的阵阵寒意……

8

A lone voice

"It's better now, the cold energy has been dissipated"

He puts away the jars, all of creation has extraordinary power

I know the ringing tones of the water drop

Are linked to all of my bones

Day after day, the rain falls incessantly

What do the hands of the blind masseur grasp

Is it a stony and deep seated fear?

9

"How does it feel right here? This spot should

Trigger your senses, between this strip of muscle

And bone there is a tenderness

That can touch your nerves, restrict

Your arms, blot out your dark nights

Don't let any drafts penetrate your body

Don't let yourself be altered by fear."

10

If pain could be transformed

Into something that had a shape, like

Grabbing a handful of salt, scattering it on the ground

Like carrying away a basin of clear water

From inside the skin, like

Wiping dirt from an apple

8

响了一夜的孤寂之声
"现在好了，寒气已经散尽"
他收起罐子，万物皆有神力
那铿锵的滴水的音律
我知道和所有的骨头有关

一天又一天雨下个不停
盲人按摩师的手抓住的
是不是那石头般的内心恐惧？

9

"这里怎样？这里应该是
感官的触动，这条肌肉
和骨头之间有一种痛
能触动你的神经，压迫
你的手臂，毁灭你的黑夜

不要让风穿过你的身体
不要让恐惧改变你。"

10

如果能把痛楚化成
有形的东西，类似
抓住一把盐，撒在地上

类似端走一盆清水
从皮肤里，类似
擦掉苹果上的污迹

Like fingers striking the keys of a piano
Then moving lightly away

11

The dance between fingers, so light
While the fingers' strength is solid, the powerful and weak
Sounds of life are all here in this moment

The blind man sits, sharing his memories
When you touch something with your hands, what the spirit
    perceives
Is truer than what meets the eyes
The accumulated things that fill your mind
Are more enduring than all that you see

12

A mass of jumbled thoughts in this material world
Melted by you in the furnace of darkness
Struck at last into one great sheet of iron

When you're ready to see, you'll be able to see
A world that has achieved tranquility
The days go by, year after year, without rest
The blind man leans over, massaging
The center of the pain, day after day

Translated by Andrea Lingenfelter

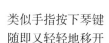

类似手指按下琴键
随即又轻轻地移开

11

手指间的舞蹈，很轻
指力却浑厚，生命中的
强弱之音此时都在

盲人坐着，细说记忆
那触手一摸，心灵的辨识
比眼睛的触摸更真实
大脑中反复重叠的事物
比看得见的一切更久长

12

尘世中的一大堆杂念
被你熔与黑暗一炉
终将打成整铁一片

当你想看，你就能看
最终达于静止的世界
日子年复一年，并不休息
盲人俯身，推拿
疼痛的中心，一天又一天

LIFE

Try hard to stay calm,
a nauseating plotline
dangling its arc light in the sky.
I ask for nothing.

The body undulates in waves
as if holding back the world's assault.
I turn it over to you,
this life full of crisis, this life that can't let go,
that beholds but never sees the daily slaughter.
So terrible, from what planet does it come?
On dry land fluids run free, unwilling to vanish.
What kind of airflow is sucked into the sky?
Such a bloated gift, such a small universe
garrisoned by grave forces.
Everything's vanishing, everything's transparent
but my most secret blood's made public.
Who threatens me?
Who tallies the undying things
others have hidden in my body,
mightier than dark night?

生命

你要尽量保持平静
一阵呕吐似的情节
把它的弧形光悬在空中
而我一无所求

身体波澜般起伏
仿佛抵抗整个世界的侵入
把它交给你
这样富有危机的生命、不肯放松的生命
对每天的屠杀视而不见
可怕地从哪一颗星球移来？
液体在陆地放纵，不肯消失
什么样的气流吸进了天空？
这样膨胀的礼物，这么小的宇宙
驻扎着阴沉的力量
一切正在消失，一切透明
但我最秘密的血液被公开
是谁威胁我？
比黑夜更有力地总结人们
在我身体内隐藏着的永恒之物？

Tears wing through warm evenings,

pitiless vessels chilling air.

Death covers me.

Death can't bear the pain that pierces all,

but don't disturb that lifeless face,

so frightening, so enchanting, as the room darkens.

Daylight was part of me once, now snatched away.

Overhead the orange light glares down at me,

staring at the world's most terrible element.

Translated by Diana Shi & George O'Connell

热烘烘的夜飞翔着泪珠
毫无人性的器皿使空气变冷
死亡盖着我
死亡也经不起贯穿一切的疼痛
但不要打搅那张毫无生气的脸
又害怕，又着迷，而房间正在变黑
白昼曾是我身上的一部分，现在被取走
橙红灯在我头顶向我凝视
它正凝视这世上最恐怖的内容

MY YOUNGER BROTHER IN THE WATER

Water   it's a room filled with waves
            it's a little bit sad
poured down from the sky into the perfume vial inside the body
I sniff the air
Catching a whiff of that chill
Seated here my beloved   Brother
To my right   a quick change of costume
O the water   has covered our toes

"I" answer as if there were a small fruit in my mouth
Spat out it drives deep as a lance
Casting a glance   bright as a jewel
It's the trail
Brother   when the summer days press down   I want to
Draw a picture of myself with flowers in my hair
The spirit of my eyes   flows out the back of the paper
Shoots into the clouds   Could anyone be
More obsessively clean than that?
O the water   has covered our heels

水中的弟弟

水　兼有一室沧浪
　　兼有一点悲伤
凌空倒进体内的香水瓶
我嗅啊嗅
嗅到分别的寒气
座中有我所爱　弟弟
在我的右侧　匆匆改了装
水呀　淹过了脚趾

"我"　回答时像含着一枚果
吐出来像深深的长矛
宝石光样的　孤注一掷
迷失了它的背影
弟弟　当夏日逼人　我愿
绘一张簪花小影
看看我眼里的气　透出纸背
射向云　能否
达到更深的洁癖？
水呀　淹过了脚踵

Our parents   a thousand miles away

Our flesh and blood   in the water

Our shoes   deep in the dust of the road

We twins

Neither freed   nor bound   shedding few tears

Helmets   and inhuman eyes

Sink to the bottom of the water   Brother

I love only those wild acres

Like an old and intimate friend

O the water   is covering our knees

A weakness for the grotesque

Like the eye of a needle   that you can't see through

And you can't know its depth   Brother

Your eyes and heart

Weeping with hunger

Tears that make the bubbles tremble   Bolt by bolt

Sunlight's fabric   startles

Listless birds flying low

O the water   has covered our waists

Brother   as winter approaches

The knife's blade is flashing   a frosty salutation

Lurking inside your gentle voice

"Will" or "Won't"

Have hurt me   In this pair of

我们的双亲　在千里之外
我们的骨肉　在水中
我们的鞋　埋在纤尘里
我们这一对双胞胎
不放纵　不拘束　甚少哭泣
头盔　还有异类目光
沉入水底　弟弟
我独爱千顷之野
如同心中旧识
水呀　淹过了膝盖

对畸形的事物嗜好
就像一个针眼　看不穿
又不知其深　弟弟
双眼和内心
都在贪馋地流泪
它们抖动泡沫　一匹一匹的
阳光布料　惊吓了
闷闷低飞的鸟
水呀　淹过了腰腹

弟弟　当冬日将至
刀刃已在闪光　冰霜的问候
躲在你的柔和嗓音里
"要"或者"不要"
伤了我　在这两叶

Burnt-out lungs   O, I

Raise high my ten unruly fingers

It's not a surrender   but an advance

Stirring up a pool of lamentations

O the water   has covered our chests

Offering libations, compiling books, losing sleep

Brother — unfathomable depths

Have tamed the past, the future and this life

They bathe   quench the lamps

And fall asleep in each other's arms   All of this

Is a question of Nature   Brother

And not of metaphysics

Nor is it simply a problem between men and women

O the water   has risen to our necks

That depth   does it move you to love

That cold   helps you

Ceaselessly probing   innocence

And zealotry   Brother

Is our nature something we inherit?

Or is it the honey that's distilled

When a poem passes by

Morning and evening we'll drink a cup   to our mutual health

In the dark our nostrils flare and breathe in

The intense sweetness…

O the water   has covered our heads

Translated by Andrea Lingenfelter

灰心的肺囊里　我呀
高举起熙熙攘攘的十根手指
不是投降　是向前
搅起一池哀嚎
水呀　淹过了胸腔

爵酒、修书、失睡
弟弟——不可测的度
驯服了前尘、后世和今生
他们洗一个澡　灭灯
然后相拥而眠　这一切
是自然的问题　弟弟
不是形而上的主题
也不仅仅是男女的问题
水呀　淹过了脖颈

那深　是否触动了爱
那冷　帮助你
对天真　对热忱
不断研究　弟弟
我们的天性是遗传?
还是诗歌路过时
派生出的蜂蜜?
早晚饮一杯　对彼此有益
黑暗中的鼻孔嗅到
那极端的甜……
水呀　淹过了头顶

STRAW

With every pull

I give a shudder

my effort

sucks the air between us dry

the straw becomes so light

too light to bear such pressure

it should be filled

with indigo liquid

if only I were farther from my own power

Translated by Andrea Lingenfelter

吸管

每吸一下
我就颤抖一次
我的用力
吸干了你我之间的空气
吸管变得如此轻
它不该被如此挤压
它应该充满
蓝色的液体
假若我离我的力量远一点

READING THE NEWS

Every night

    he comes across

        news of some awful murder

(dismembered corpse   suicidal granny   poisoned hotpot)

        — just then he's flooded with the desire for sleep

        these horrifying stories

        have numbed every square inch of his skin

Let me tell you:

my wife is a thrill-seeker

the universal gravitation of her body

plummeting suddenly

The heating power of sulphur and placer gold

scream from the crowns of our heads

bullets crazily pinching   the weight of our arms

        every evening amidst this

terror and joy we reach

ecstatic peaks   the phone rings "hello"

will gold and the case of the dismembered corpse

explode in concert?

Translated by Andrea Lingenfelter

读报

每天晚上
    他读到
        一则凶杀新闻

（碎尸案　奶奶的自杀　毒血旺）
      ——此刻他睡意高涨
    那些令人敬畏的消息
    麻醉了他的每一寸肌肤

让我告诉你：
我的妻子是一个冒险家
她体内的万有引力
陡转直下

硫磺和砂金的热力
在我们头顶呼啸
子弹疯狂地夹紧　双臂的重量

      每个晚上　我们
在欢欣和恐惧中达至
极乐巅峰　"喂"的电话声
黄金和碎尸案会不会
一同爆炸？

DISGUISE

(When I lick a hole in the paper window
this bathroom fills my eyes)

I see a woman
doing some things
She opens her eyes wide   lets her hair down
Facing the mirror   she uses a sea sponge
to scrub her entire body
as if shaving off her own fish scales
The strange thing is   she uses her own hands
to set her head down
Now   she paints her own brows
(How can she   treat her own body
as if it's formless
How can she
dismember herself
as if dismembering   a man's muscles and organs?)

Drop by drop   the bathroom water
flows out of the room   drop by drop
flows downstairs   drop by drop
flows into the street

画皮

（当我把一扇纸窗棂舔破
这个浴室就装进我的眼里）

我看见一个女人
做一些事情
她把眼睛睁大　头发散开
对着镜子　她用海绵
擦洗全身
好像在刮自己的鱼鳞
奇怪的是　她用自己的手
把她的头端下
现在　她为自己画眉
（她怎么可以　像对待无形般
对待自己的躯体
她怎么可以
像肢解男人的肌肉　器官一样
肢解自己）

浴室里的水　一点点
流到室外　一点点
流到楼下　一点点
流到大街上

Those trees   those bricks

the concrete ground

have already been informed

that my fear-filled love

has changed into fear

and now slowly spills out from inside my body

I will continue loving

and will love my fear   When I see

she wash her body clean

then put powder-capsules into her skull

it's as if she's putting white onto her skin

Since she looks brand new

she becomes more powerful   Her demons

her poison   her sharpness

return to her body drop by drop

This is how I watch myself

slowly lose yang energy

It flows out slowly

This is how I don't think of saving myself

and continue experiencing pleasure

Until death, I won't be clear

which one I loved:

the bewitchingly made up one   the embodied one

or the you I discovered

after having washed away the poison

Translated by Jami Proctor Xu

那些树　那些砖
那些灰色水泥地
已被告知
我的充满恐惧的爱
变成恐惧
正从我体内慢慢溢出

我将继续爱
也爱我的恐惧　当我看见
她洗净了自己的身体
把一些药末装进头颅
好像把白色装进皮肤里
既然她焕然一新
更有力量　她的魅
她的毒　她的锋利
一点点返回体内

我就是这样看着自己
慢慢地失去阳气
慢慢地流了出去
我就是这样不思自救
继续我的快意

到死我都不清楚
我爱的哪一个？
粉妆蛊惑　肉身的
还是洗净了毒素
被发现的你？

2000.8.21

DAYLIGHT SLUMBERS

These are our daylight slumbers

        he says, right now we're looking up

        our necks have no other purpose

        besides kissing   sucking

the mirror, the comb and naked heels

hinge upon their points

        the two halves of a whole body

        one half inscribed: day

        the other: night

(calling you   a child of nature

calling you to help me prop up this summit)

outside the window

        a tower crane falls towards me

        I toss and turn   but cannot shut my eyes in sleep

Translated by Andrea Lingenfelter

白日之眠

这是我们的白日之眠
　　　他说，这时头朝上
　　　脖子一别无他用
　　　除了亲吻　吮吸

镜子，梳子和赤裸的脚后跟
弯下了它们的尖状
　　　全身的两半
　　　一半写着：昼
　　　一半写着：夜

（称呼你出自自然
呼你　助我直抵峰巅）

窗外
　　　塔吊高高向我落下
　　　辗转睡去　也无法闭上双眼

THE BIG DREAM'S A DRAMA

The big dream's a drama

where light bursts onto darkness.

At the end of the performance,

the audience leaves their seats,

each furrow of despair

blooming into life.

Translated by Diana Shi & George O'Connell

大梦如戏

大梦如戏
当光涌入黑暗
如散场时人们纷纷离席
意识从每一折绝望里
栩栩地活过来

LIES

43 muscles cross our faces,

ten thousand moods.

Science, once I grew up, said so.

Each day's thousand phrases

hide a hundred lies.

Each day, my lie detector,

you find mine.

Translated by Diana Shi & George O'Connell

谎言

我们的 43 块肌肉
可以激起脸上的上万种表情
这是我成年后读到的科学数据

每天，上千句话语中
有一百句谎言
每天，你是我的测谎仪

FOR LÜ DE'AN

Someone left a letter on my desktop
— in the middle of a New York blizzard
just as I was using an inch of crayon
to pencil in half-inch wide eyebrows
and third-inch wide American-style eyes
(typically larger than Chinese eyes)

and as for our poems
they don't rain down and bury you like big puffs of goose down
turning us white   disguising us
as beautiful interludes in each small town

in my hometown (and in yours too)
they're seldom seen   when they do appear
they're front page news
so very fine, they swirl and drift, borne slowly aloft
so many winters   but they are still as rare
and precious   as poetry

Translated by Andrea Lingenfelter

给吕德安

有人把信送到我的桌前
——正当纽约大雪时
我正在用一寸炭精条
挑出 0.5 寸的眉毛
以及 0.3 寸的美国式眼睛
（一般比中国人大）

至于我们的诗
却不像落满你全身的大片鹅毛
把我们变白　伪装成
各个市镇的美丽时光

在我的家乡（你的家乡也一样）
它们不常见　偶尔来临
因此要上报纸头条
它们细细飘零慢慢起飞
冬天那么多　它们却那么少
因此弥足珍贵　跟诗一样

TRYING TO DRAW

Just drawing a happy scene
Just drawing the relationship you both have with air
and your movements, like mother and son

To begin with, I want to draw diligently
not half-heartedly
I want to draw for my own climax
and not for someone else's

Poor tender creatures
They don't think this way
When they draw, they're just drawing some poses,
drawing some peaches, pears, and bananas
They get the consideration they deserve

Look at all those yuppies
and workaholics   You're so outstanding
But don't tell me about all your
various feelings
If you're worn out
go feel sorry for fading fragrance and pity jade
You'll definitely succeed

试着去画

也就是去画一种　快乐情景
也就是去画　你与空气的关系
你们的跳动　好像母与子

首先我想认认真真地画
而不是马虎地画
是为自己的高潮而画
不是为别人的

年轻娇嫩的小可怜
她们并不这样想
她们画　也就是画一些体态
画一些桃子　李子和香蕉
她们得到应有的照料

放眼望去　那些雅痞士
工作狂　多么优秀
但别向我　倾诉你们的
情感种种
你们累了
就去怜香惜玉吧
你们肯定成功

What I'm trying to master

is a certain quality of time

One that doesn't see its head   doesn't see its tail

Incomparable lightness

combed from my short hair

Strand by strand, it lengthens, deepens

Trying to draw   I notice

the intricacy and importance of breathing

the incomparable slightness   and movements of the body

Trying to draw   I place particular emphasis on

the loss and inability to recover light

I have been a molecule of every substance

My passivity   has already reacted with other matter

It certainly wasn't fatal

Trying to draw   trying not to need

Trying to shake my head at time

Trying to say "no" to some people:

my body will be light as a swallow

Translated by Jami Proctor Xu

我试着掌握的
是一种品质时间
它们不见首　不见尾
无比轻逸　从我的短发上梳理起
它们一根根地变长，变深

试着去画　就注意到
呼吸的细小和重要
身体的无比轻微　和运动
试着去画　就侧重于
光线的失去　和无法打捞

我曾是所有物体的分子
我的消极　已与其他物质反应
它将不是致命的
试着去画　试着不需要
试着对时间摇头
试着对一些人说"不"
就会身轻如燕

　　　　　　　　　　1999.8.18

I'M DRUNK AND YOU'RE DRY

The glass arrives right on time
you're not drunk   but who'd want to
grasp so treacherous a vortex?
and what's the point, anyway?

The instant smiles I see
are so faint   so intelligent
because I'm awash in my own drunkenness

Every kind of alcohol fears me
that's why nighttime   is best
for going out on a limb   for snatching from drunkenness
that chemical reaction   you know well
my perfume   and know even better
each and every glance I've stolen

Suddenly I'm flushing red
but you get bluer all the time
if it isn't alcohol   it must be
a wound
shoring up the strength
your sobriety softly sucks away

我醉，你不喝

杯子如约而来时
你不醉　那谁肯
握住一个险恶的漩涡
还有它的必然？

我所看到的突然的微笑
那么小　那么聪明
是因为我埋在醉里

所有的酒精都怕我
因此夜晚　最值得
蹈入险境　去取走醉里的
化学反应　比熟悉我的
香水品牌　你还熟悉
我偷走的每一道目光

突然我慢慢变红
而你也变得更蓝
如果不是乙醇　那就得
是一个伤口
它们补充你被不醉
轻轻吸走的功力

Love is like wine
some breathe its   vapors while others imbibe
and bring it into existence   and let it draw blood
and bring us pain   only intoxication
let us place our faith in another's folly

Right now I want it to be like life itself
and not just an accessory to living
but what can I nurture it with?
drugs, food, sex?

The effect I was impatient for
gives a round of applause

I'm turning into a lush
a half-inch of liquor away from the bottom of the glass
you're not drinking, and I get drunker all the time

Translated by Andrea Lingenfelter

爱如同酒
有人闻它　有人饮
它才存在　它才滴滴见血
才让人心痛　才会在醉里
相信某个人的怪念头

现在我要它像个生命
而不只是生活的附件
我用什么来养它？
药物，食物，性物？

我不愿等待的后果
已开始鼓掌

终究要变成红人了
0.5 寸高的酒要就见底了
你不喝，我醉得更快

FIREWORKS AND WORKING GIRLS

Fireworks and working girls
They've danced with abandon
Descending into loneliness in the end

A moralist would not agree:
Their explosions in the heavens are natural
We watch as we please   reflect as we please
On newly illuminated   corners once overlooked

If my will could ascend to the sky
I'd want to go to pieces too
In the quest for love   I'd dance a proud dance
Anyone might   surrender to lust beneath the moon
Even the moon adores its own ecstasy

If it were able
It would light its own fuse
Every flowery bone of its body
Scattering to the winds

Translated by Andrea Lingenfelter

烟花的寂寞

烟花与烟花女子
都有过狂欢起舞
最终，她们落入寂寞

道学家们不会同意：
她们在天上的爆破多么自然
我们随便看　随便想
就被照亮了　不曾经意的角落

假如我的意志也可以升空
我也想四分五裂
为了求爱　笔直起舞
每个人都会　对着月亮狂乱
月亮也酷爱自己的极乐

假如可能
它也会引爆自己
从每一个方向
洒出全身的花朵骨头

EBB TIDE

This evening, facing the south mountain,
I sit at its foot, coat open,
the whole lake a sorcerer's potion
quickening the mind.

Yesterday, today, tomorrow
someone tastes the nameless pain
coursing through the body, an egg
bulged on the plate, shrinking as one eats,
a slug of nourishment pulsing in the flesh.

Yesterday, today, tomorrow
it remains: call it consciousness,
however it shifts form,
rising at first light,
flooding our organs,
sinking at blue dusk,
time's cholesterol.

退潮

有一个黄昏我披襟向南山
坐于山脚　看看：
整个湖水变成迷药
锐化了我的意识

过去、现在和将来
都有人感受到无名的痛楚
漂浮在体内　像刚烘热的鸡蛋
缓缓凸起　又在盘中下沉
那一堆养料在体内循环

过去、现在和将来
它都存在：被叫做"意识"的东西
虽然它一变再变
虽然它在晨曦中高涨
漫过五脏六腑
在暮色下退去　变成时间的胆固醇

Blood, saliva, sap of plants,

all that nature feeds

to bless the body's core,

shattering the stones of impatience.

See how the falling sun, grown fat

on your insomnia,

sets so early. Yet its rusty light

dissolves the gloom within my chest.

Cold starlight sharpens thought.

Go and dance the art that quells

the tumult of the nerves.

Translated by Diana Shi & George O'Connell

血液、唾液和植物汁液
所有来自自然的食物和物质
都给身体的能量中心加持
化掉因急躁而结成的顽石

看看：夕阳因你的失眠
而变重变沉
已经提早落下
胸中块垒也被落日的铁锈溶掉
星辰的冷光　仍在锐化我的意识

现在去舞踏　一种功夫可以治愈
运动神经的骚乱

2012.9.28

NATURAL ENEMIES

Violently, from the sky, he
hurls himself down

I adjust my glasses and look
up, a pair of silhouettes

hers, armored
as ever in night

he turns her
into something rigid

because
they are natural enemies

I persist in twisting
on paper   these words

it's evolving into a fatal game of cat and mouse
now   I'm even smaller than they are

and I wonder if my natural enemy
is not faith itself

Translated by Andrea Lingenfelter

天敌

他，猛地，从空中
摔下自己

我抬了抬眼镜
看见，两条身影

她的，盔甲
一向是黑夜

他把她变成
僵硬的一条

因为
他们是天敌

我继续蜷缩在
纸上　那些字

渐渐变成猫与鼠的厮拼
现在　我比它们更小

不知道我的天敌
是否相信

THINGS ARE ALWAYS LIKE THAT

Some dreams   unlike beautiful dreams
Are all about motorcycles
Gas stations and mayhem
Like the violent movies we're used to watching

They're always flying around
Their kind of violence
Is at once gentle and grandiose
Like an aesthetic

They're naked   they're excited
Beneath white sheets
Wild   or tender
Light as cranes' feathers
They make a pledge   whenever they talk they'll talk about love
Are they convincing themselves   or trying to convince each other
Tonight I've started to wonder

Things are always like that
Beautiful or not   they're always the same
Entering our brains
Always standing together in the same way
Dragging us down

它们总是如此

有些梦　不同于很美的梦
关于摩托车
加油站和蹂躏
类似我们看惯的暴力片

它们总是这样飞来飞去
它们这些暴力
它们总是又温柔又铺张
像一个美学

他们赤裸　他们兴奋
他们在白色床单下
狂野　或者温柔
都轻如鸿毛
他们发誓　他们言必称爱
他们在说服自己　还是对方？
这一夜产生了怀疑

它们总是这样
美与不美　它们总是这样
进入我们的大脑
它们总是这样站在一起
把我们毁掉

The sun shouldn't be jealous

Of the rays of light beneath it

The sun shouldn't shine

On the realities that encircle beauty

Some dreams   always reveal their murderous intent

For in the dark of the moon

They'll always become classics

Like the violent movies we're used to watching

Things are always like that

They bump around in the dead of night

And speak for the bones in our bodies

If delight were as vast as that

They would speak for our doubts as well

You can kill without meaning to make it a habit

Swallow poison without thinking of death

Fall in love and never wonder what the year might bring

Translated by Andrea Lingenfelter

太阳不应该嫉妒
它之下的一切光芒
太阳不应该照亮
围绕美的全部事实

有些梦　总是杀机毕现
盖过月黑的时候
总是成为经典
类似我们看惯的暴力片

它们总是这样
它们在黑夜里嘎嘎生长
它们代表我们身体的骨骼
要是欢爱如此巨大
它们就代表我们的怀疑

杀人时不会想到有瘾
就像下毒时不会想到死
爱人时也不会想到明年今天

A WORD

A guy taught me a word
He divided it into: a term used in bed
a term used in life   and a term used in books
That guy didn't know
when I used it   I closed off its attributes
the same way I gush out tears
but close my tear ducts

This word exists in the world unknown to me
but it screams inside my body
I know how shrill its scream is   I know
it is faster than the speed of wind   But I don't know
where its explosions—heavier than air—
are going to take me

Too many guys have taught me this word
And I've taught them this word's transformations

Translated by Jami Proctor Xu

一个词

一个男孩教给我一个词
他把它分为：床上用语
生活用语　书面用语
那个男孩不知道
当我使用它　我关掉了它的属性
就像我喷出眼泪
却关掉它的液囊

世界上有这不为我知的词
它却在我的身体里发出尖叫
我知道这尖叫有多高　知道它
快于风的速度
却不知道　它重于空气的发作
要将我带到什么地方

我使用它　就像机器使用它的性能
太多的男孩呵，教给我这个词
而我　教给他们这个词的变化

2000.8

CHRYSANTHEMUM LANTERNS GO FLOATING BY

Chrysanthemums go floating by, dot after dot

Through the darkness   through the enclosing silence

Past the muffled voices of children by the river

Pale chrysanthemums   paleness startling the shadows of birds

Children holding lanterns float slowly by

In their shallow singing

There is no fear   no play   no pain

Only chrysanthemum lanterns   the paleness of chrysanthemums

The crimson of lanterns

And young ladies holding lanterns float slowly by

Young ladies and their servants

Hair tied in loose knots

All of their finery is nothing but

Satin sashes and buttons

Nothing but jingling and jangling

Tassels   earrings   phoenix hairpins

The young ladies and their nursemaids

They're passers-by

They're seeking in their leisurely way

A midnight rendezvous with the moon

The girls are gentle the lanterns gentle too

They float, o they float

They turn an ordinary night

Into an extraordinary walking dream

210

ZHAI YONGMING: SELECTED POEMS

菊花灯笼漂过来

菊花一点点漂过来
在黑夜　在周围的静
在河岸沉沉的童声里
菊花淡　淡出鸟影

儿童提着灯笼漂过来
他们浅浅的合唱里
没有恐惧　没有嬉戏　没有悲苦
只有菊花灯笼　菊花的淡
灯笼的红

小姐也提着灯笼漂过来
小姐和她的仆从
她们都挽着松松的髻
她们的华服盛装　不过是
丝绸　飘带和扣子
不过是走动时窸窣乱响的
缨络　耳环　钗凤

小姐和小姐的乳娘
她们都是过来人
她们都从容地寻找
在夜半时面对月亮
小姐温柔　灯笼也温柔
她们漂啊漂
她们把平凡的夜
变成非凡的梦游

Every night

Chrysanthemum lanterns float slowly by

The master of lanterns   wanders far and wide

No one can keep up with

His uneven pace, now fast now slow

The children grow up in his footsteps

This is the tale of a lantern on the deep blue sea

If I were sitting on the floor

I would feel afraid of that breath of power

I would feel afraid of those blossom shadows   light shadows

human shadows

And I would give voice, now fast now slow

Ringing like a bell in the room

Sitting on the sofa or the bed

It would put me at ease

And I'd feel myself slowly turning translucent

Slowly changing color

Holding the smoke inside me all night   And then

I'd float up from the ground

Translated by Andrea Lingenfelter

每天晚上
菊花灯笼漂过来
菊花灯笼的主人　浪迹天涯
他忽快忽慢的脚步
使人追不上
儿童们都跟着他成长

　　这就是沧海一灯笼的故事

　　如果我坐在地板上
　　我会害怕那一股力量
　　我会害怕那些菊影　光影　人影
　　我也会忽快忽慢
　　在房间里丁当作响

　　如果我坐在沙发或床头
　　我就会欣赏
　　我也会感到自己慢慢透明
　　慢慢变色
　　我也会终夜含烟　然后
　　离地而起

CLIMBING THE HEIGHTS ON THE DOUBLE NINTH

— PEOPLE ALL AROUND ADORNED
WITH FLOWERS, BUT SOMEONE IS MISSING

The problem of longing for family   the problem of brotherly love

The most touching problem of all is

Climbing the heights

When you've reached a pinnacle

And raise a cup

Today I am alone   who is there to talk to?

Taking in a distant view   what people call the North Bank

Is that a single white ribbon joining the River, or are there two?

Wherever those twined currents   go I'll be content

Beyond the North Bank   are beautiful women without number

Every man who climbs these heights   will think of them

Even if in the next thousand years   mammals

And humans   merge into one

Maintaining the balance of Nature

Today I raise a cup alone   while River and mountains change color

The green months of spring depleted me

This figure, "Nine Nine" is once again

Reborn in my veins

Faraway peaks above and below

Plunge naked into my heart

It's useless but all I can do is to

Enjoy the glorious sunshine

重阳登高

——遍插茱萸少一人

思亲问题　友爱问题
一切问题中最动人的
全部是登高的问题
都是会当凌绝顶时
把盏的问题

今朝一人　我与谁长谈?
遥望远处　据称是江北
白练入川是一条，还是两条?
汇向何处　都让我喜欢

在江北以远　是无数美人
男人们登高　都想得到她们
尽管千年之内　哺乳动物
和人类　倒一直
保持着生态平衡

今朝我一人把盏　江山变色
青色三春消耗了我
九九这个数字　如今又要
轮回我的血脉
远处一俯一仰的山峰
赤裸着跳入我怀中
我将只有毫无用处地
享受艳阳

Longing is miserable   Being drunk is miserable too

How many sighs in the soughing of the wind?   Who will answer

   my echo?

Wine poured down the throat   flows into the body's deepest reaches

Problems of desire and mortality

Problems of separation and health

Also change inside the throat   and flow into the body's deepest reaches

They become nimble   yet meticulous

They're drunk   and they're everywhere

Translated by Andrea Lingenfelter

Zhai Yongming notes that she wrote this poem after climbing Xisha Mountain in Nanjing on the Double Ninth. The Double Ninth is a festival that takes place every autumn, on the ninth day of the ninth lunar month. The original meaning of the festival may have been related to driving away bad luck, but it has long been an occasion for outings, especially hikes in the hills to some viewpoint, for chrysanthemum viewing, and for drinking chrysanthemum wine. Traditionally, people also wore zhuyu flowers on this day, for good luck. The epigram is taken from a poem by the Tang dynasty poet, Wang Wei (699–759 CE), "Missing My Shandong Brothers on the Ninth Day of the Ninth Month" . (九月九日忆山东兄弟) .

思伤脾　醉也伤脾
飒飒风声几万？　呼应谁来临？
饮酒入喉　它落到身体最深处
情欲和生死问题
离别和健康问题
也入喉即化　也落到最深处
它们变得敏捷　又绵密
它们醉了　也无处不在

IN ANCIENT DAYS

In ancient days, I'd only
write letters, not knowing
where we'd meet.

Now I flood your email,
my characters like stars
chasing after you.
I care little where they land.

In ancient days, mountains were green facts.
Blue water at our feet,
we'd simply clasp fists, keeping faith
we'd meet again.

Now you fly this place and that,
my small stars trailing through the sky,
reaching out as to a sore spot,
countless tries to patch
the blue screen, though not hysterical.

在古代

在古代　我只能这样
给你写信　并不知道
我们下一次
会在哪里见面

现在　我往你的邮箱
灌满了群星　它们都是五笔字形
它们站起来　为你奔跑
它们停泊在天上的某处
我并不关心

在古代　青山严格地存在
当绿水醉倒在他的脚下
我们只不过抱一抱拳　彼此
就知道后会有期

现在　你在天上飞来飞去
群星满天跑　碰到你就像碰到疼处
它们像无数的补丁　去堵截
一个蓝色屏幕　它们并不歇斯底里

In ancient days, how many poems

to be a Lao Shan Taoist, to slip into

a cup of bamboo-leaf tea,

stride on air, pass through brick walls

and seize you. Or

beat one's head bloody.

Now, you thumb a phone

that wafts ten thousand scents,

the fragrance of a distant body.

One part trembles and a whole world shakes.

Ancient days weren't like this.

We spurred the horses then, side by side,

covering a few miles.

My earrings clinked, a grin showed on your face.

We kept our heads down, and rode.

Translated by Diana Shi & George O'Connell

Lao Shan: Mt. Lao, near Qingdao on the Shandong coast of E.
China, is one of the "cradles of Taoism."

在古代　人们要写多少首诗?
才能变成崂山道士　穿过墙
穿过空气　再穿过一杯竹叶青
抓住你　更多的时候
他们头破血流　倒地不起

现在　你正拨一个手机号码
它发送上万种味道
它灌入了某个人的体香
当某个部位颤抖　全世界都颤抖

在古代　我们并不这样
我们只是并肩策马　走几十里地
当耳环丁当作响　你微微一笑
低头间　我们又走了几十里地

2004.5

THE LANGUAGE OF THE '50S

Born in the '50s   that's the language
We speak
These days   it's the stuff of stand-up
At dinner parties   where it's served
Line by line

Those red flags, leaflets
Violent images   those
Belts pulled taught by stalwart thumbs
And those bloodthirsty slogans   have been brought down hard
The victimizers and victims
Are gone for good
The love of an entire generation   has been castrated
Gone for good

Born in the '50s   but
We'll never use that language again
Just as we'll never say "love" again
Every act of speech, each phrase and tone
Capers about yellowed with age at dinner parties

五十年代的语言

生于五十年代　我们说的
就是这种语言
如今　它们变成段子
在晚宴上　被一道一道地
端了上来

那些红旗、传单
暴戾的形象　那些
双手紧扣的皮带
和嗜血的口号　已僵硬倒下
那些施虐受虐的对象
他们不再回来
而整整一代的爱情　已被阉割
也不再回来

生于五十年代　但
我们已不再说那些语言
正如我们也不再说"爱"
所有的发声、词组和语气
都在席间跳跃着发黄

None of them understands   their youthful hair

Shines multicolored in the sun   like soap bubbles

Floating beside us

They bow their heads in unison

Their thumbs busier than their other digits

Texting on QQ and there's a symbolic typography too:

Born in the '50s

We too need to learn   that language flying around the ether

All of those vanished words

Lived at a particular time

Like the grapes, wolf berries and dates scattered on our marriage bed

They fall between the sheets

And when I murmur   speaking each word one by one

My boyfriend understands   and they

Turn the vivid red of blood

Translated by Andrea Lingenfelter

他们都不懂　他们年轻的发丝
在阳光下斑斓　像香皂泡
漂浮在我的身边
他们的脑袋一律低垂着
他们的拇指比其他手指繁忙
短信息 QQ 还有一种象形字母：
生于五十年代
我们也必须学会　在天上飞奔的语言
所有那些失落的字词
只在个别时候活过来
它们像撒帐时落下的葡萄、枸杞和大枣
落在了我们的床笫之间
当我喃喃自语　一字一字地说出
我的男友听懂了　它们
因此变得猩红如血

BIDIS

Xi Chuan hands me a bidi
the same kind of cigarette he smoked ten years ago

Bidis aren't Xingjiang tobacco
but they taste just like it
recalling a low-class sexiness

The poets smoke bidis
imagining this is the smell of poor people's shacks
In fact   we're staying in the diplomatic quarter
with views of lush, verdant grounds   green peacocks pacing
huge, black crows
flapping towards the round conference table and a magpie chattering

We're ashamed   not only because our writing is pallid
not only because everyone else is speaking Hindi   Thai
Chinese or Bengali
not only because we're discussing religion & nationalism

So many questions, all constantly being translated
while people from all walks of life are picking up bidis
taking a drag, inhaling
finally exhaling
ring by ring, driving away the smell of a politicized soil

Translated by Andrea Lingenfelter

Xi Chuan [tk]
Bidis are a kind of cheap cigarette popular among India's poor. They are made
of N. rustica, rather than the less potent N. tabacum, which is most commonly
used in cigarettes.

毕利烟

西川递给我一支毕利烟
十年前他抽过的毕利烟

毕利烟不是莫合烟
但如同莫合烟的味道一样
充满低层人民的性感

诗人们抽着毕利烟
想象这是贫民窟的味道
实际上　我们住在使馆区
窗外绿茵如织　绿孔雀踱步
乌鸦大而黑
扑向讨论圆桌上的"乌鸦嘴"

我们感到羞愧　不只是写作苍白
不只是用印度语　泰语
中国语或孟加拉国语
不只是讨论宗教问题　民族国家问题

如此多的问题不断被翻译
就像毕利烟不断被不同阶层的人
叼起、抽着、吸进
最后吐出来
一圈一圈去政治化的本土味道

SAD SUBMARINE

Nine AM. At the office.
Coffee. Pen and ink.
Check the weather outside.
My sub and I, useful or not,
must be on watch, its lead gray hull
afloat in the still harbor. At first

I wanted to say
now that war's less likely
and curses grown mild,
but when I listen close
I hear the clink of silver.

I crave scarlet seafood,
how in hard times its redness glows.
Hands that master information
busily stuff our maws.
When I started writing this, I saw
lovely fish besieging the shipyard,

The jumbled ledgers of state-owned firms,
the flat economies of neighboring states,
hookers' painted faces.
Fake receipts
circle the shallows.

潜水艇的悲伤

九点上班时
我准备好咖啡和笔墨
再探头看看远处打来
第几个风球
有用或无用时
我的潜水艇都在值班
铅灰的身体
躲在风平的浅水塘

开头我想这样写：
如今战争已不太来到
如今诅咒　也换了方式
当我监听　能听见
碎银子哗哗流动的声音

鲜红的海鲜　仍使我倾心
艰难世事中　它愈发通红
我们吃它　掌握信息的手在穿梭
当我开始写　我看见
可爱的鱼　包围了造船厂

国有企业的烂账　以及
邻国经济的萧瑟　还有
小姐们趋时的妆容
这些不稳定的收据　包围了
我的浅水塘

So I write instead

better go check the sub

before it enters deep water, and wonder

whose blood vessel will shelter it.

Pop star fans, hippies, disco heavy metal,

periscopes that filter words.

Alcohol, nutrition, high calories—

prepositions, pronouns, interjections

fix the texture of my skin.

The sub must plunge

beyond control

to the bottom of the sea.

I said once already:

you build your own submarine,

war's monument,

a tomb that will slumber

forever at the bottom of the sea

in service to solitary and remote moods.

As you see, assembly's finished.

But where's the water,

and which shore does it lap?

Now to build my own ocean

from each thing's

impeccable sadness.

Translated by Diana Shi & George O'Connell

于是我这样写道：
还是看看
我的潜水艇　最新在何处下水
在谁的血管里泊靠
追星族，酷族，迪厅的重金属
分析了写作的潜望镜

酒精，营养，高热量
好像介词，代词，感叹词
锁住我的皮肤成分
潜水艇　它要一直潜到海底
紧急　但又无用地下潜
再没有一个口令可以支使它

从前我写过　现在还这样写：
都如此不适宜了
你还在造你的潜水艇
它是战争的纪念碑
它是战争的坟墓　它将长眠海底
但它又是离我们越来越远的
适宜幽闭的心境

正如你所看到的：
现在　我已造好潜水艇
可是水在哪儿
水在世界上拍打
现在　我必须造水
为每一件事物的悲伤
制造它不可多得的完美

　　　　　　　　　　　1999.9.18
　　　　　　　　　　　2000.9.21

AT THE NORTH SIDE OF THE PARK

At the North side of the park, a ghost
sings day and night:
"I am dead, please bring me back to life
so that I may become a living person, anyone!"

At the North side of the park, a passer-by
stops, looking around:
"Who is that? Who is it that
speaks these senseless words?"

At the North side of the park, friend Lili
returns home in a hurry:
"It's too much, too much sadness
with which friend can I speak?"

At the North side of the park, Qiong's husband
wags the paintbrush to make a picture:
"The birds glide though the sky
how can I glide through these thoughts?"

公园以北

公园以北，一个鬼魂
正昼夜歌唱：
"我死了，请让我复活
成为活着的任何人"

公园以北，一个行人
正停足四望：
"是谁？又是谁？
在说着这些疯话？"

公园以北，女友莉莉
正匆匆回家：
"太多了，太多的伤心事
对哪位朋友讲？"

公园以北，琼的丈夫
正挥笔作画：
"鸟儿飞过天空
我怎样飞过这些思想？"

The unjustly dead ghost has a vulnerable soul

asks: why no will to compromise?

The passer-by, in a hurry, thinks in his heart:

The only peaceful place is the grave!

Lili, on the floor below, studies the flowered Chinese fabrics

the mirror forgets its own limits

from above, Qiong's husband caresses the canvas

Qiong thinks: these colors are the ones that kill

Translated by Claudia Pozzana & Derek Bermel

冤死的鬼魂心灵脆弱
它在问：为什么不肯让步？
匆匆行走的人在心里想：
坟墓才是太平的地方！

莉莉在楼下研究中国花布
镜子遗忘了自己的限制
楼上，琼的丈夫触摸麻布
琼在想：这些谋杀般的颜料

CENTRAL PARK

On such an afternoon   much longer than morning
Much hotter than summer
Hyper-white bodies collapse on the burning grass
Lili n Qiong carry a drawing board under their arms
Their penetrating eyes float incessantly

A man passes by   not romantic enough
Another man passes by   not really sentimental
So many men with a well-fed face
Pass through Central Park   pointed out one after the other

Lili sets up the drawing board   lifts her chin
The landscape like a painting   nothing has changed
She cannot but think of those inevitable years
Lili's heart under the white transparent silk dress
Jumps up and down? Qiong's heart
Stretches out towards Lili's fingers
Fingers tapered like stems
Burning, raising the problem of Lili's existence

A piece of charcoal dances   the face of Qiong emerges
Where can one realize happiness's purpose?
To understand, only to understand where to buttress
Half the heart's rivers and mountains
How worn Qiong's face is!

中央公园

在那样一个下午　比上午长得多
比夏天热得多
白花花的躯体倒在炎热的草地
莉莉和琼挟着画板
熟透的眼睛变幻不定

一个男人走过　不够浪漫
又一个男人走过　不太伤感
多少个男人营养过剩的脸
走过中央公园　被一一指点

莉莉支起画板　抬起下巴
江山如画　什么也没改变
不能不想起那无法躲过的几年
莉莉的心在白色透明的丝裙里
跳来跑去……琼的心
正倾向莉莉的十根手指
葱管似的手指
迫切竖起莉莉存在的问题

炭条飞舞　出现琼的脸
幸福的指标在何处兑现？
懂得，仅仅是懂得在支撑
内心的半壁河山
多么憔悴琼的脸！

Now in front of her eyes

A pretty woman has been drawn

Sitting though agitated   and also

A woman devoured by ambition

With red hair and rosy cheeks   jumps off of the paper

So perfect as to astonish

Also drawn is the livid white of the starving

The multicolored skin covered with sores

On such an afternoon

much longer than morning

Much longer than days torn out from the calendar

Imagine Lili and Qiong

Entering the park's safe center

Translated by Claudia Pozzana & Derek Bermel

现在正是眼前：
画过一个窈窕淑女
坐立不安　又画过
一个野心勃勃的女人
红发美颜　从纸上跃起
完美和令人感叹
也画过饥饿者的青白
各色皮肤的遍体鳞伤
在那样一个下午
比上午更长
比撕去日历的日子更长
设想莉莉和琼
已步入公园审慎的中间地带

THE SONG OF HISTORICAL BEAUTIES

Sitting in a tea garden with a friend one day
Our talk turned to Kaiyuan and Tianbao
That gilded age
Those days of chaos and strife

When I was young
I searched high and low for things to write about
I wrote of war, of women's loneliness
And about hardships that came together like an awl
Piercing my memory
And I write and write, writing myself into middle age

I saw the entire thing
That night, the 15th of the lunar month:
A girl dancing on a platter
A pair of shadows swaying in the breeze
Surrounded by admirers —
The eaves inclining towards her
Golden chrysanthemums wafting the scent of all creation towards her
The West wind lifting her skirt and then

Someone nearly hidden
Transfixed by her dancing legs

时间美人之歌

某天与朋友偶坐茶园
谈及，开元、天宝
那些盛世年间
以及纷乱的兵荒年代

当我年轻的时候
我四处寻找作诗的题材
我写过战争，又写过女人的孤单
还有那些磨难，加起来像椎子
把我的回忆刺穿
我写呀写，一直写到中年

我看见了一切
在那个十五之夜：
一个在盘子上起舞的女孩
两个临风摆动的影子
四周爱美的事物——
向她倾斜的屋檐
对她呼出万物之气的黄花
鼓起她裙裾的西风　然后才是

　　　那注视她舞蹈之腿的
　　　几乎隐蔽着的人

Under a full moon, I watch it all

Unquestionably real

A dancing girl with flowers in her hair

She dances, the moonlight seeming to pass right through her

She dances, movement flowing up from the bones in the soles of her feet

She dances, sweeping away the fallen leaves

(She gives no thought to palace intrigues

Desiring only to dance with the wind, to dance with the wind)

Surrounded by hungry eyes and

The admiration of all creation

Watching as her flesh is laid bare

Very few people remember

What I wrote about

When I was young

I wrote of illness, of childhood

My darkest days and all their troubles

In my misery, I looked down on this mundane world

And I wrote and wrote, writing myself into middle age

I can say I've witnessed scenes of warfare:

Smoke swallowing the sun, blades piercing the sky

The generals' standards half furled, dirges filling the air

Why do we hear such mournful songs outside the tent?

月圆时，我窥见这一切
真实而又确然
一个簪花而舞的女孩
她舞，那月光似乎把她穿透
她舞，从脚底那根骨头往上
她舞，将一地落叶拂尽

（她不关心宫廷的争斗
她只欲随风起舞、随风舞）

四周贪婪的眼光以及
爱美的万物
就这样看着她那肉体的全部显露

当我年轻的时候
少数几个人还记得
我那些诗的题材
我写过疾病、童年和
黑暗中的所有烦恼
我的忧伤蔑视尘世间的一切
我写呀写，一直写到中年

我的确看到过一些战争场面：
狼烟蔽日，剑气冲天
帅字旗半卷着四面悲歌
为何那帐篷里传出凄凉的歌咏？

A glass of wine is poured into a shining amber cup

A woman dons her soft Persian armor

What makes the general's eyes fill with tears?

What makes that peerless beauty quake in fear?

(She gives no thought to the neighing of the emperor's horses,

Wanting only to be with him, to be with him)

Tonight, apart from the ancient moon

And a chill wind that raises the hairs on the back of my neck,

Who else is there? Eyes fixed on this mound

Of images of spilled blood and broken bones

When I was young

I had so many ideas that never saw the light of day

I've written of love, of longing and

The steady gaze of a man   The only thing I haven't written

    about is growing old

Writing and writing, writing myself into middle age

Some miles westward they ride, to hot springs in the hills

To soak in that faintly fragrant water

A silk gown folded on the ground

Some miles westward they ride, reining in their mounts to a halt

War-weary officers and men call out for blood

There's always someone in the shadows, denouncing women for their crimes

一杯酒倒进了流光的琥珀酒盏
一个女人披上了她的波斯软甲
是什么使得将军眼含泪花？
是什么使得绝代美女惊恐万状？

（她不关心乌骓马嘶鸣的意义
她只愿跟随着它，跟随他）

除了今夜古老的月亮以及
使我毛发直竖的寒风
还有谁？注视着这一堆
淤血和尸骨混合的影像

当我年轻的时候
我丢下过多少待写的题材
我写过爱情、相思和
一个男人凝视的目光　唯独没有写过衰老
我写呀写，一直写到中年

西去数里，温泉山中
浮动着暗香的热汤
一件丝绸袍子叠放在地上

西去数里，勒马停缰
厌战的将士一声呐喊
黑暗中总有人宣读她们的罪状

Some miles westward they ride, and as they flee

The moon weeps with them

A jade hairpin tumbles to the ground

(She doesn't hear the rumble of war drums shaking the earth

She hears the unbroken flow of whispers, unbroken strings of oaths)

Legions of soldiers and thousands of horses have trod past these springs

Their waters are as warm as ever, and just as sweet

Love after death, and love newly born

Well up from that source, as they always have

I was sitting with a friend in a tea garden one day

And our talk turned to how swiftly golden ages come and go

I'll never be young again, never again be so willful

As to pit one half of creation against the other

I watch with wonder the flurry of people and things as they come and go

Time has neither paused nor stopped, not for any of them

I keep on writing, just as I always have

And these are the lines I wrote:

西去数里，逃亡途中
和泪的月光
一根玉钗跌落在地上

（她听不见动地的鼙鼓声
她听见绵绵私语，绵绵誓）

千军万马曾踏过这个温泉
那水依然烫，依然香
后世的爱情，刚出世的爱情
依然不停地涌出，出自那个泉眼

某天与朋友偶坐茶园
谈及纷纷来去的盛世年间
我已不再年轻，也不再固执
将事物的一半与另一半对立
我睁眼看着来去纷纷的人和事
时光从未因他们，而迟疑或停留
我一如既往地写呀写
我写下了这样的诗行：

"One night, under a full moon

They abandoned themselves to passion

Leaving their bodies limp to the core

Men, oh men

At first they praise a women for her beauty

But at other times

When cities erupt in flames

Men, oh men

Delight in denouncing women for their crimes"

Translated by Andrea Lingenfelter

The Kaiyuan era corresponds to the years 713–741, during the reign of Tang Xuanzong.
The Tianbao era spanned the years 742–756, during the reign of Xuanzong.
Tang Xuanzong (685–762) reigned from 712 to 756.
This poem alludes to three legendary and historic beauties: Zhao Feiyan (c. 32 BCE–1
BCE), an empress of the Western Han; Yu Ji (died 202 BCE), consort of Xiang Yu of
Chu; and Yang Guifei (719–756), consort of the Tang Emperor Xuanzong. All three
women were vilified by traditional historians.

"当月圆之夜
由于恣情的床笫之欢
他们的骨头从内到外地发酥
男人啊男人
开始把女人叫做尤物
而在另外的时候
当大祸临头
当城市开始燃烧
男人啊男人
乐于宣告她们的罪状"

THE GECKO AND I

There you are,

faithful to the ceiling,

your eyes threatening even in the liquid dark.

How many times

my heart's shuddered at your gaze,

soundless, still,

a silence so fearful

I flee the room.

When my spirit's high,

I nearly forget you.

When I have a drink,

as night's silk falls on my shoulders,

my striding legs feel elegant.

But when I see you,

shy, mild thing,

I lose my way.

You stare, I stare,

our gaze locks

Across an abyss, alien souls

who'll never know

the other's pain.

The nest of your dreams

can't be the desert of my heart,

yet both cast their shadows on the wall.

壁虎与我

你好！壁虎
你的虔诚刻在天花板上
你害人的眼睛在黑暗中流来流去
我的心灵多次颤栗
落在你的注视里
不声不响一动不动
你的沉默如此可怕
使我在古老房间里奔来跑去

当我容光焕发时
我就要将你忘记
我的嘴里含着烈性酒精香味
黑夜向我下垂
我的双腿便迈得更美
我来到何处？与你相遇
你这怕人的温驯的东西
当你盯着我我盯着你
我们的目光互相吸引

异邦的心灵
隔着一个未知的世界
我们永远不能了解
各自的痛苦
你梦幻中的故乡
怎样成为我内心伤感的旷野
如今都双重映照在墙壁阴影

How long have I slept? Meeting you

stuns me helpless.

Some strong hands might dare

your touch, but those tiny paws

chill me more than a monster's.

Move, gecko, move.

Translated by Diana Shi & George O'Connell

我死了多久？与你相遇
当我站在这儿束手无策
最有力的手也敢伸出
与你相握那小小的爪子
比庞然大物更让我恐惧
走吧壁虎的你

1992

致谢　　　本诗选里的诗是由 Andrea Lingenfelter、Diana Shi、George O'Connell、Wang Ping、Lewis Warsh、Jami Proctor-Xu、Claudia Pozzana、Derek Bermel、顾爱玲等著名翻译家译成英文，谨致谢忱！

图书在版编目（CIP）数据

翟永明诗歌英译选 / 杨四平主编. —— 上海：上海
文化出版社, 2023.3
（当代汉诗英译丛书）
ISBN 978-7-5535-2689-8

Ⅰ.①翟… Ⅱ.①杨… Ⅲ.①诗集—中国—当代—汉、英 Ⅳ.
①I227

中国国家版本馆CIP数据核字(2023)第027517号

出 版 人：姜逸青

责任编辑：黄慧鸣　张　彦

装帧设计：王　伟

书　　名：翟永明诗歌英译选

主　　编：杨四平

出　　版：上海世纪出版集团 上海文化出版社

地　　址：上海市闵行区号景路159弄A座3楼 201101

发　　行：上海文艺出版社发行中心

　　　　　上海市闵行区号景路159弄A座2楼 201101 www.ewen.co

印　　刷：苏州市越洋印刷有限公司

开　　本：889×1194 1/32

印　　张：8

印　　次：2023年6月第一版 2023年6月第一次印刷

书　　号：ISBN 978-7-5535-2689-8/I.1035

定　　价：58.00元

告 读 者：如发现本书有质量问题请与印刷厂质量科联系 T：0512-68180628